She'd never in her life seen such fierce hunger.

Such concentrated intensity.

Travis had moved her. Affected her. Diana had realized it almost from the very moment she'd met him. She'd vowed to suppress the attraction. Extinguish it completely. But it kept rekindling itself, like the embers of some smoldering fire that were fanned and brought back to blazing life by its very presence.

And she'd been certain that he, too, had meant to crush any visceral urges he might have. She'd witnessed his determination to deny the attraction he felt.

What she was feeling was only a whim. A whim that could be conquered. That *would* be suppressed.

Otherwise, both their lives were bound to change forever....

***

SINGLE
DOCTOR
DADS

Don't miss any of the heartwarming stories in Donna Clayton's **SINGLE DOCTOR DADS** series:

Dear Reader,

There's something for *everyone* in a Silhouette Romance, be it moms (or daughters!) or women who've found—or who still seek!—that special man in their lives. Just revel in this month's diverse offerings as we continue to celebrate Silhouette's 20th Anniversary.

It's last stop: STORKVILLE, USA, as Karen Rose Smith winds this adorable series to its dramatic conclusion. A virgin with amnesia finds shelter in the town sheriff's home, but will she find lasting love with *Her Honor-Bound Lawman*? *New York Times* bestselling author Kasey Michaels brings her delightful trilogy THE CHANDLERS REQUEST… to an end with the sparkling bachelor-auction story *Raffling Ryan*. *The Millionaire's Waitress Wife* becomes the latest of THE BRUBAKER BRIDES as Carolyn Zane's much-loved miniseries continues.

In the second installment of Donna Clayton's SINGLE DOCTOR DADS, *The Doctor's Medicine Woman* holds the key to his adoption of twin Native American boys—and to his guarded heart. *The Third Kiss* is a charmer from Leanna Wilson—a must-read pretend engagement story! And a one-night marriage that began with "The Wedding March" leads to *The Wedding Lullaby* in Melissa McClone's latest offering.…

Next month, return to Romance for more of THE BRUBAKER BRIDES and SINGLE DOCTOR DADS, as well as the newest title in Sandra Steffen's BACHELOR GULCH series!

Happy Reading!

Mary-Theresa Hussey

Mary-Theresa Hussey
Senior Editor

Please address questions and book requests to:
Silhouette Reader Service
U.S.: 3010 Walden Ave., P.O. Box 1325, Buffalo, NY 14269
Canadian: P.O. Box 609, Fort Erie, Ont. L2A 5X3

The Doctor's Medicine Woman

DONNA CLAYTON

SILHOUETTE *Romance*®

Published by Silhouette Books

America's Publisher of Contemporary Romance

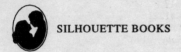

SILHOUETTE BOOKS

ISBN 0-373-19483-8

THE DOCTOR'S MEDICINE WOMAN

Copyright © 2000 by Donna Fasano

This edition published by arrangement with Harlequin Books S.A.

Visit Silhouette at www.eHarlequin.com

Printed in U.S.A.

DONNA CLAYTON

is proud to be a recipient of the Holt Medallion, an award honoring outstanding literary talent, for her Silhouette Romance *Wife for a While*. And seeing her work appear on the Waldenbooks Series Bestsellers List has given her a great deal of joy and satisfaction.

Reading is one of Donna's favorite ways to wile away a rainy afternoon. She loves to hike, too. Another hobby added to her list of fun things to do is traveling. She fell in love with Europe during her first trip abroad and plans to return often. Oh, and Donna still collects cookbooks, but as her writing career grows, she finds herself using them less and less.

Donna loves to hear from her readers. Please write to her care of Silhouette Books, 300 East 42nd Street, New York, NY 10017.

Travis Westcott, M.D.
Family Practice
Philadelphia, Pennsylvania

Patient File

Name: Me

Diagnosis: Lovesick Single Doctor Dad

Symptoms: Rapid pulse, difficulty concentrating....long, sleepless
               nights

Prescription: Kiss a certain Kolheek Medicine Woman senseless!

Travis Westcott
Physician's Signature

Chapter One

"We have decided to permit the adoption—"

Travis Westcott felt pure and utter joy rush through his body as he stood before the Kolheek Council of Elders.

"—but there is one, very small—" the speaker paused, her bronze, wizened face showing little emotion "—catch."

His stomach lurching with sudden suspicion, Travis couldn't keep the dismay from his voice as he repeated, "Catch?" His brow furrowed, his head tilting a fraction. "What sort of catch?"

He'd worked so hard to prove himself worthy to these people. He'd traveled from Philadelphia to the northern Vermont reservation four times over the past two months in order to appear before the Council to plead his case, to explain to the Elders that his single status would not keep him from being a good father to the five-year-old twin brothers, Jared and

Josh. And just when he thought the boys would be his, he was being presented with yet another obstacle, yet another mountain to climb. He couldn't help but worry how high and steep this one might turn out to be.

"Dr. Westcott," a second member of the Council of six men and women spoke up, "maybe we shouldn't say 'catch.' The word has such an underhanded connotation attached to it. What we should say is *stipulation.* And please know that this... condition was decided upon with our best intentions and the boys' best interests in mind, we assure you."

"The boys' best interests were all that ever concerned me." Irritation tinged his quiet tone, cloaking Travis's fear of disappointment. Becoming the twins' father had become so important to him. More important than he'd ever imagined.

"If this has something to do with the fact that I'm not married," he said. "I've already explained—"

"No." The first Elder shook her head.

Travis couldn't believe that the state and federal governments of the United States had no say in this matter. But he'd learned that the Kolheek were totally in control of who did or did not adopt the orphans from their small tribe. The Council had complete authority in the matter.

"This has nothing to do with the fact that you cannot provide the boys with a mother."

Guilt swept through him when he heard the situation voiced in those terms. He'd thought he could give the boys everything they needed by way of a parent. Resolve made his spine straighten. He *could* give Jared and Josh all they needed. He was certain of it. And if this catch, this stipulation, they were suddenly presenting him with, didn't have to do with his marital status, then the Council, too, thought he could give the boys all they needed.

Then what? he wondered. What was this condition they were hinting at?

Patience, he silently chided. If he'd learned nothing else over the months of dealing with the Native Americans, he'd learned that they revealed their thoughts, plans and opinions in their own good time. No matter what kind of hurry or rush anyone else might be in.

"You've made your arguments," the elderly woman said. "You've convinced us that you will love the boys. Provide for them. And the fact that you are half Kolheek only served to help your cause. You showed us just how much you cared by seeing to it that the boys were provided with the medical attention they needed two years ago. Their heart conditions might have killed them were it not for your intervention, Dr. Westcott. We know all these things."

The second Council Elder continued, "The boys will be six soon. And you know that with each day, each week, each month that passes, their chances of being adopted diminish. It is a sad but true fact that couples want to adopt impressionable babies, not adolescents already on their way to being grown. We *want* you to adopt Jared and Josh. We believe the three of you will make a happy family. If we didn't, you wouldn't be here today."

"Then what is it?" Travis leveled a steady gaze

on the group, his impatience thinly, if at all, veiled. "What's the catch?"

Attempting to intimidate the Elders was futile. It was apparent that these people had lived long, full lives. They had endured hardships, pain and sorrow the likes of which he would never know. They had experienced happiness, laughter and tranquillity. These six men and women were the dignitaries of their tribe. Only the oldest and wisest could sit on the Council. Their vast life experiences showed in their proud faces. In the set of their shoulders. In the unmistakably enlightened glints of their dark, deep-set eyes.

"There is no easy way to present the problem we see," the woman told him. "We find it disturbing to know that you will be taking the twins far from the reservation. Far from their home. Far from The People."

Travis frowned, finding her words quite alarming. "But you knew from the beginning that I lived in Pennsylvania. You don't expect me to move here to Vermont? Here to the reservation? I have a medical practice in Philadelphia..."

She shook her head in silent answer, somewhat calming his rising panic. "But we are concerned that the boys will lose touch with their heritage. Their past. Their ancestors." Her voice grew soft and gentle as she added, "Dr. Westcott, you are ignorant in the ways of The People."

Although he realized that the woman tried to relay her concern without insulting him, he bristled at what felt like an ugly criticism. Ignorant was not a word that would normally describe him. He was a successful physician. Co-author of a textbook widely used by medical colleges all over the world. He was a sought-after speaker at conventions and seminars. Because of his dogged determination and his knowledge of the workings of the human body, he'd saved lives. As these facts rolled through his head, Travis knew he wasn't being conceited. He was simply being honest about himself and his accomplishments.

However, if he were to continue being honest, he'd have to concede to the Council woman's criticism. For her observation was true. He knew nothing of his Native American heritage.

His mother, a full-blooded Kolheek, had left the reservation as a teenager when she'd married his father. She had never returned. She had gladly adopted her husband's culture, his religion, his whole way of life. And she had never attempted to reveal anything about her Indian background to her two sons. Even after her bitter divorce, Lila Westcott had never returned to the reservation. Travis had grown up thinking of himself as nothing more than a...proud American.

"I love those boys." He silently thanked heaven that his voice didn't break with the tremendous emotion welling inside him. The idea that he could lose the chance to be their father distressed him mightily.

He wasn't used to making himself vulnerable to others, but at this moment he felt it was necessary. He could think of no other response to the woman's accusation. He did love Jared and Josh. And he planned to be the best father he could be. He wanted to give them everything. But how could he give them something he didn't have? He couldn't offer the boys knowledge of the past when he didn't know it himself. He couldn't furnish them with the wisdom of a culture of which he was unfamiliar.

The old woman's eyes softened in her wrinkled face. "We don't doubt your deep affection for the children, Dr. Westcott. We know you will feed and clothe them. We know you'll provide them with a safe home, a good education. With tremendous emotional support." She inhaled, her chin lifting a fraction. "But we feel they need more."

"Due to their medical condition, they have lived in a state orphanage," the second Council member added. "Like you, they know little to nothing of their heritage, of the Kolheek ways. They need a link to their past. And we've found just the person who can give them that. Our Medicine Woman."

Diana Chapman sat in the waiting area outside the Council room. The last thing she wanted to do was spend two months in the home of Dr. Travis Westcott—*single* Dr. Travis Westcott.

But her grandmother, the senior member of the Council Elders, had asked Diana to make this trip, to prepare a set of five-year-old twin boys for their naming ceremony, as a personal favor. Diana had been taught to grant all her Elders the utmost respect, and she'd have at least considered the request no matter which Council member had approached her. But she loved her grandmother dearly. She'd move heaven and earth if doing so would please the woman who had raised her.

Diana knew that the doctor was a successful man. Someone who could afford to raise and educate the young twins. A man who took his responsibilities seriously. And he was half Kolheek. These had been the facts that had swayed the Council to allow their own to be adopted by someone living off the reservation.

But the thing that concerned Diana was Travis Westcott's single status. With her heart barely mended from her difficult divorce, she didn't relish the thought of being cooped up in a house with a man who was most probably "on the hunt." Since returning to the reservation ten months ago, she'd been pursued by every bachelor within the reservation boundaries, and even some outside them. She'd turned down more date invitations than a Christmas turkey had feathers. Why couldn't men take no for an answer without getting their pride all knocked out of joint?

Her grandmother had told Diana that her worry about suffering the doctor's attentions was like interest on a loan she may never owe. Then the woman had gone on to assuredly say that she felt Diana could handle herself in any situation. "If the need arises, simply be honest with the man," her grandmother had suggested. "Just as you've been with the others."

So Diana had decided to do just that. She'd help Jared and Josh, and she'd do her best to steer clear of Travis Westcott.

However, she couldn't help but wonder how the doctor was going to react to the Elder's condition of having a Medicine Woman live in his home for a while. Men were strange creatures who didn't take very well to ideas that weren't their own. Diana's

mouth quirked up at one corner. Her grandmother—
amazing woman that she was—would convince him
that the stipulation was necessary, Diana was certain
of it.

Just then the door opened, and she was summoned
into the Council room.

The air was thick, and one look at Travis Westcott's face told her he wasn't happy. He wasn't
happy at all. But even with a frown marring his high,
intelligent forehead, she couldn't help but recognize
that he was a handsome man. A *very* handsome man.

Surprisingly, her knees turned rubbery and her
stomach churned as if it had been invaded by a slew
of fluttering butterflies. This anxiety bewildered her.
Was she worried because the man was so obviously
irritated? Or because he was so startlingly handsome?

What nonsense, she silently chided. She stood a
little straighter. Never again would she be intimi-
dated by an angry man. Or a handsome one, either,
for that matter.

His displeasure seemed tempered, even if only for
a moment, as his jet-black gaze perused her face.
Something lit in his eyes. Surprise? Appreciation?
Interest? Mere curiosity? Diana couldn't tell. But she
felt her mouth draw into a hard line. She refused to
be concerned with his curiosity, his appreciation *or*
his interest, and she immediately averted her gaze,
focusing her attention on the Council members. More
specifically, her grandmother.

"Dr. Westcott," her grandmother said to the doctor, "I'd like you to meet my granddaughter, Diana
Chapman. Diana, Dr. Westcott."

The doctor met her halfway and reached out to shake her hand.

His grip was firm and warm and…secure.

She had to force herself not to step back in surprise at the thought. Why would that descriptive term come to mind? But she didn't have time to linger over the unsettling question.

"Please," he said to her softly, "call me Travis."

She offered him a professional smile. "Only if you'll call me Diana."

He nodded, holding onto her hand for what she felt was a little longer than necessary. Then every inch of her skin prickled with awkwardness and her palm felt distinctly chilled when contact between their hands was broken.

"Congratulations on the successful adoption of Jared and Josh," she said.

"Thanks." He then added, "I think."

Was the aside his attempt at good-natured teasing? she wondered. His own self-doubt? Or was he rebelling against her presence being forced on himself and the boys?

"I'm not sure yet that the adoption *is* successful," he said.

"Be assured—"

Diana looked toward the Council table as her grandmother spoke to Travis.

"—the adoption is complete. Now that you have agreed to accept Diana's help, we are happy to release the boys to you."

The doctor's immense happiness seemed to fairly pulse from him, Diana observed. But the frown on his brow quickly returned.

"For how long?" he asked.

The Council, as a whole, looked confused by his question. But it was Diana's grandmother who continued to speak on their behalf.

"Forever," she told him. "Or at least until Jared and Josh reach maturity."

"No, no," he said. "I wasn't referring to the boys. Um…no offence to Ms. Chapman—"

"Diana," she softly reminded him. Surely they could be on a first name basis and still act professionally toward each other.

At her prompt, his mouth curled slightly at the corners as he cast her a quick glance, and Diana got the nerve-racking and overwhelming sense that, if this man were to ever truly smile at her, his face would be transformed from merely handsome to utterly and breathtakingly gorgeous.

He directed his gaze at her grandmother. "Just how long will I be expected to…" His words trailed into a brief and awkward pause. He tried again. "How long will Diana be with me and the boys?"

The elderly woman nodded her understanding. "In two short months the boys will turn six. It is the Kolheek tradition to hold a naming ceremony on—or close to—a child's sixth birthday."

Diana watched Travis shake his head.

"Naming ceremony? But the boys already have names."

"Kolheek names," the Council woman explained.

Knowing she could clarify in a way he would understand, Diana offered, "Long ago, the infant mortality rate was very high. Parents discovered it was best to wait—"

"That is the rationalization given by cultural professors at colleges and universities." Diana's grandmother enunciated the words with gentle but firm disapproval. "The real reason is that the Kolheek believe a child should have the chance to develop a personality before he is gifted with a name."

A patient smile tugged at the corners of Diana's mouth. This wasn't the first time she and her grandmother had clashed over her academic cultural studies of the Kolheek people.

"Had you given me a chance, Grandmother, I'd have explained fully."

"I know you would have," her grandmother granted. "But the day is quickly passing. And surely the good doctor is anxious to collect his children."

Now Travis was smiling. At the Council. Diana could sense the warmth of it, but because she stood slightly behind him and to one side, she could not see his face and was only left to wonder if her thoughts about how a smile would transform his features was true or not. Somehow, she felt deprived.

When next her grandmother spoke, the woman's voice was louder, more formal than it had been just a moment before, and Diana knew an edict of the Council was being declared.

"Our Medicine Woman will live with Dr. Westcott and the boys until such time as she deems them ready to be named. She will teach the children all she can of the Kolheek and the essence of what it means to be part of The People. She will prepare Jared and Josh for their naming ceremony, and she will perform that ceremony." After the very briefest of pauses, she added, ''Then we shall see what fate has in store.''

Diana shot her grandmother a curious glance. What on earth had she meant by that last peculiar statement?

The flight back to Philadelphia was packed with business travelers and vacationers, but Travis paid little attention to his fellow passengers—except the two young boys sitting beside him. Jared and Josh were craning to see out the small window on what was so very obviously their first trip in an airplane. Jared chattered away excitedly, while Josh just seemed to silently take in everything with his huge, dark eyes.

All Travis had to do was look at the boys and his chest swelled with pride, his heart with paternal love. He'd thought the fatherly feelings would take time to develop, that becoming the boys' daddy would have to grow on him. However, he'd discovered rather quickly when he'd picked up the children at the orphanage this afternoon just how wrong he'd been.

Jared and Josh already knew Travis as he'd been to visit them twice a year since arranging their operations—and more often since he'd started the adoption process—so that made the meeting less stressful for everyone concerned. Upon being told that Dr. Travis, as the boys had referred to him until now, was taking them home to live with him, the boys' reactions had made Travis's heart literally ache with throat-closing emotion.

Jared had grinned and seemed to accept the situ-

ation eagerly. He'd asked if Travis was really going
to be his daddy. The question had made Travis nearly
strangle with the surprising magnitude of love that
surged through him. He hadn't been able to answer
with anything other than a silent nod.

Josh's reaction had been poignant, too, but in a
very different way. His silence was profound, his
large, chocolate eyes shadowed with some emotion
Travis couldn't quite identify, but that he suspected
was suspicion. And fear. Travis had wanted desperately to comfort the boy, embrace him, assure him
there was nothing to be afraid of. However, he'd
been worried that becoming physical too soon would
only compound the child's fear. Trust would come
in time, Travis was certain.

The child's misgivings were abated somewhat
when Jared had tossed his arm over his brother's
shoulder and had said, "It's going to be okay, Josh.
You'll see."

Although Jared's chin had lifted with what looked
like much bravado, Travis hadn't missed the anxiety
lacing the boy's reassuring remark. He'd wanted to
hug the boys to him, to tell them they needn't worry
another second, that he'd move mountains to see that
they were loved and well cared for. But he'd stifled
the urge, silently noting again that trust—like
Rome—wasn't built in a day.

The boys' meager belongings had been packed
into one suitcase and they had spent a tearful half
hour saying goodbye to the friends they'd made at
the state home and the staff there that had cared for
them for the first five years of their lives. Travis had
patiently given the children as long as he could be-

fore telling them they had to get on the road to the airport.

At the mention of airplanes and runways, Jared had come alive with excitement. Josh did his best to underplay his feelings about all this commotion, but Travis knew the child was just as eager for this new experience as his brother.

As he now watched the boys press their faces against the small, double-paned window, Travis sighed. The trip to the reservation had been pretty close to perfect. He'd come home with the boys...

The sigh he now expelled was filled to the brim with doubt and agitation. He wasn't really angry that he'd had to agree to Diana Chapman's presence in his home for the next couple of months. He agreed with the Kolheek Council's opinion that Jared and Josh needed some roots. They were young. And impressionable. They needed a sense of heritage. A heritage that Travis couldn't give them because he didn't have it himself.

He looked across the aisle at the woman's arrow-straight, black-as-midnight hair, her tawny skin, noble cheekbones, perfect nose.

What was it about Diana Chapman that unsettled him so? Was it because she was a Medicine Woman? Someone living the very culture he was so totally ignorant of? Or was it because she had been forced on him? Because she was someone he'd see as an invader in his house? In his new family? *Or,* a quiet voice silently stressed, was it because she was too darned beautiful for words?

She turned her head, her nut-brown eyes connecting with his, and she caught him staring for what seemed the umpteenth time since they'd boarded the plane. Awkwardness crept over him, thick and straining. What was it about her that made him feel so…rough and unrefined? Ham-fisted, even?

Her dark, steady gaze was trained on him, and he felt the silence swell and grow even more awkward than it had been only a moment before. The urge to reach up and tug at his collar welled up in him like an unreachable itch, but he firmly squelched it.

Her quiet dignity, her almost patrician manner, was what had him feeling so damned uncouth.

Say something, you idiot, his brain silently poked him like a stick. *Say something that will bridge this difficult stillness.*

"So," he began, hating the dry-as-dust sound of his voice, "tell me…what exactly does a Medicine Woman do?"

Diana went utterly still. When she had left the reservation in order to attend college in southern California, she'd shied away from telling anyone in the outside world that she was training to become a Kolheek Medicine Woman. The title was archaic to the modern world. And to people who weren't familiar with Native American culture, the term often provoked snickers and thinly disguised jeers.

She remained silent for several seconds as she tried to decipher whether the doctor's query had been prompted by disdain or honest curiosity.

He hadn't said much to her since they had left the reservation together and traveled to the nearby small town of Iron Hill, Vermont, to pick up the boys at the state orphanage. Diana had pretty much stayed in the background as Travis happily broke the news to

Jared and Josh that the adoption had been successful, that they would be going home with him. To stay.

Jared had been all smiles, but Josh had taken the information in silence. Over the next half hour or so that they were at the home, Diana watched in silence as Travis interacted with his new sons. The only introduction she'd received was that she was a 'lady from the reservation who'll be staying with us for a while.' She hadn't minded being brushed over. Travis had only told the truth, and it was important that the focus of the moment be placed on the boys, who needed to understand the change that was about to take place in their lives now that they had been adopted by Travis.

The trip to the airport was filled with Jared's questions. The child wanted to know how big the plane would be, how high they would fly, if they'd be above the clouds, if they'd eat a meal. His questions had rung like the peals of a high-pitched bell. Travis had remained patient, and that had impressed Diana.

Finding no guile in Travis's eyes now, Diana said, "It would probably be easier to tell you what a Medicine Woman *doesn't* do."

He obviously recognized her quip for what it was—an attempt to reduce the strain between them. He smiled, and Diana's breath literally caught in her throat. She'd been right. His smile really did change his already handsome features into a countenance that stole away all thought. For a moment her mind went blank, her heart raced, as she took in his even, white teeth, the smile lines around his mouth and eyes. My, but he was a handsome man.

"Jack-of-all-trades, are you?" he said, interrupting her chaotic thoughts.

She blinked, struggling to calm her jangling nerves, her racing mind. What had they been talking about? Taking a deep, soul-soothing breath, she swiftly gathered her composure.

Her job. That was it. He'd asked about her responsibilities.

"I do…everything. I lead celebrations. I pray for the sick. I council alcoholics, unwed mothers and couples whose marriages are in trouble. I deliver babies. I diagnose illness and prescribe medication—"

"You deliver babies? And prescribe medicine?"

"Yes," she answered. One corner of her mouth pulled back a bit. "Well, the babies would come with or without my help. And the medication I prescribe is in the form of herbs, mostly. I'm what you would call a holistic healer. I'm an N.D. Doctor of Naturopathy. Certified by the state of Vermont."

"You're a bona fide doctor?"

There was no hint of derision in his tone, and for that Diana was relieved. She nodded.

"Wow, I didn't realize."

Did she hear apology in his words?

She couldn't stop the grin that took over her face. "Please don't tell me you were expecting a peace pipe and a feather headdress."

Her gentle teasing seemed to ease the awkwardness that hung between them.

"Don't get me wrong," she continued. "I have ceremonial paraphernalia. Brought it with me, in fact. For the ceremony. But I don't use it on a daily basis."

His breathy chuckle was so soft she barely heard it. "I have to admit, when the Council said Medicine Woman, I had no idea what to expect."

"Usually a Kolheek Shaman is—"

"Don't you mean Sha-*person?*"

The wisecrack was only voiced to make her laugh, she realized that.

"I've never concerned myself too much with political correctness," she told him. "And I'm not radically into feminism, either." Seeing his surprised expression, she pointedly added, "Living among the Kolheek tribe has taught me exactly which sex wields the power."

His smile waning, Travis seemed momentarily unsure of the meaning of her statement. Diana liked the idea of keeping him on his toes and made no effort to explain her thoughts further.

"Normally," she said, "I would become the apprentice of another Shaman. I would have learned everything I needed to know without leaving the reservation. But I wanted more. I wanted a formal education. And my grandmother agreed. So I attended college, and then medical school."

"What if your grandmother hadn't agreed?"

Diana lifted one shoulder slightly. "That wouldn't have happened. My grandmother is a wise woman. She knows there is very little opportunity on the reservation. We already have two family physicians. It's a small tribe. Too small to support three doctors. She knew I would someday have to find another path to follow."

"A different path? You're thinking of quitting—"

"No, no," she assured him. "I am a Kolheek

Medicine Woman, first and foremost. I will remain on my chosen path. But if I'm to support myself, it will someday take me to a different place. Off the reservation.''

"I see." He glanced over to check on the boys, and then his dark gaze leveled on her once again. "How do you feel about that? Leaving your home? Your grandmother?''

Diana averted her gaze for an instant. She moistened her lips, and tilted up her chin as she told him, "I love my grandmother dearly. She raised me. But all baby birds must someday leave the nest, fly on their own, isn't that so?''

She'd left the nest once. She'd married and thought she'd made a home for herself in California. But then she'd been wounded, she'd fled back to the reservation, her heart ripped and torn to shreds, her wings broken and bleeding.

"Sounds like you and your grandmother are very close.''

"Yes," she answered softly. She would miss her grandmother this holiday season. But Diana was determined to make her grandmother proud by doing right by the twins. Jared and Josh would know what it meant to be Kolheek when she was through. She could take great pride in that.

A frown bit into his brow as if something worrisome had just then entered his mind. "Maybe you can help me to understand something. Can you tell me what she meant today? Your grandmother, I mean. With that cryptic parting phrase she gave me? The one about fate? And seeing what it had in store?''

The sudden anxiety clouding Travis's gaze had a startling effect on Diana. Empathy enveloped her like the warm blanket of sunshine that covers the New England mountains each summer.

Travis continued, "She wouldn't let me bring the boys home, get them settled, only to deny me the right to adopt them after your stay, would she?"

His distress turned to raw fear, and Diana thought her heart would surely rend in two. And in that instant, bells and whistles sounded in her head, red warning flags waved furiously. She had no business caring so much about this man's reactions to her grandmother's words. No business whatsoever.

Chapter Two

Then we'll see what fate has in store.

Her grandmother's words had flitted through Diana's head more than once since she'd left the reservation with Travis. She remembered the unsettled feeling the obscure yet seemingly momentous statement had stirred in her as she stood with Travis before the Council.

Diana's first thought had been that the remark had been meant for *her* benefit, and she'd been bewildered by what message her grandmother might be trying to relay to her. But hearing Travis's doubts regarding her grandmother's intentions now had Diana wondering if maybe he was right. Maybe her grandmother had been issuing some kind of warning to Travis about the boys. That did make more sense. But if this was so, then it was a cruel thing for her grandmother to have done to Travis. The man was trying to do something good here. Something honorable and compassionate. Now he was being made to worry about having the twins taken from him after opening his home—*and his heart*—to Jared and Josh. Would her grandmother have done something so unkind?

Sympathy for Travis pained Diana's heart. He needed reassurance. She could tell from the expression on his face, from the doubt shadowing his intense, black eyes.

"To my knowledge, the Council has never retracted a promise," she told him softly. "And they did make you a promise today. They said they wanted you and the boys to become a family. To the Kolheek, a person's word means everything—honor, pride, honesty, integrity. A person's character is only as good as his or her word. I cannot believe…"

Her voice faltered and then trailed away as she tucked her bottom lip between her teeth. As much as she wanted to assure him, she refused to tell him anything other than the full and honest truth.

After expelling a resigned sigh, she said, "But I cannot mislead you. This situation is far different than any I've ever experienced. The Council is concerned about the boys. About their living away from their culture. About your being single." She sighed. "Until the adoption papers are signed by each Council member and the documents are in your hands, then…I would suppose that anything is possible."

"Great." His utterance was soft, more to himself than to anyone else.

Again, compassion squeezed her in its tight grip. "The Council did say they wanted you to have the boys."

"Only two of the members actually spoke," he reminded her.

"They were the Council representatives. They spoke the thoughts of everyone. If even one member had disagreed, you can be sure he or she would have spoken up."

Gratitude tinged his tone as he murmured his appreciation. She smiled at him, her stomach suddenly feeling all giddy and…and strange.

Just then a plastic drinking straw from one of the boys' sodas came flying over Travis's head, landing on the blue carpeted aisle separating Travis's and Diana's seats. Automatically she reached down to pick it up. After quietly warning the boys to settle down, Travis turned back to her and took the straw from her.

The pads of his fingers were warm as they gently brushed the backs of hers. A chill shimmied up her arm, churning up gooseflesh, and she shivered. She darted a glance at his strong hand, and then again at his handsome profile. Luckily Travis was in motion, swinging back around to speak to the twins, and he didn't seem to notice her astonishing response to his touch.

She curled her fingers into a fist and stuffed her hand into her lap. Reacting to Travis was the very last thing she wanted to do. She didn't want to be affected by him. Men were the cause of too much pain. Too much humiliation. Her only goal on this trip was to spend time with Jared and Josh, to acquaint them with their heritage. If she could help assuage Travis's doubts and fears about the adoption, she would. If she could help the boys feel more comfortable with their new father, she'd do that, too. But she didn't want any involvement with Travis other than what was necessary for the boys' sake.

Okay, so she found him handsome. Any woman would. His onyx eyes were appealingly intelligent, his long, neat hair glossy and inviting, his sexy mouth sent sensuous ideas flitting through her mind—

She cut the thought to the quick. Her body was only reacting to his good looks. This was mere physiology. She was smart enough to know that.

The steward ambled by, instructing passengers to return seats to the full, upright position and gathering used napkins and empty soda cans in preparation for landing. But Diana barely heard, so involved was she in her thoughts.

The fact that she'd identified her attraction to Travis early was a good thing. She gave a mental nod. A very good thing. What she was experiencing was a completely natural response. Purely physical in nature…hence, totally controllable if she remained vigilantly cognizant of it.

Diana glanced over at Travis, but saw only the back of his sleek, dark head, his broad shoulders and the full length of his back as he snapped young Jared's seat belt securely into place.

Controllable, she firmly thought. *What I'm feeling is totally controllable.*

The boys were so excited. They had explored every inch of the house and yard as soon as they'd arrived home. Travis had been lucky several years ago in finding an old stone manor house on a large piece of property thick with trees. A perfect setting in which to raise children, although he hadn't had that in mind when he'd purchased it. The last thing Travis had thought he'd ever have was a family of his own. He was a dyed-in-the-wool bachelor. And quite naturally, as a man without a wife, he'd never contemplated having children.

Until six months ago.

During one of his visits with the twins—a visit planned only to check on their medical condition, take them out for a meal and buy them some clothes and a few toys—Travis had heard murmuring among the staff at the state home. Phrases like ''getting beyond adoptable age'' and ''special needs children'' and ''undesirable'' kept popping up.

The orphanage administrator had told Travis they were even thinking of splitting the boys up in order to find them homes. That thought had disturbed Travis, and it had got him thinking…about becoming the boys' daddy himself, about taking them into his own home.

His friends and partners, Greg and Sloan, had thought he was crazy when he'd first voiced his idea of becoming an adoptive dad to the Native American twins. But Travis had prevailed. Something about the rambunctious boys, something about what seemed to be turning into a dire situation for them, kept calling to Travis. Wouldn't leave him alone. He had been meant to raise these boys. He could feel it in the very pit of his gut. He might not have been able to find the right words to make anyone fully understand his feelings, but he knew it in his heart. Thank the good Lord above, he'd been able to clarify his feelings to the Kolheek Council well enough that they had allowed him to bring the boys home with him to Philadelphia.

And as he listened to the thumps and bumps coming from the upstairs bedroom, he smiled to himself and knew he hadn't made a mistake. Jared and Josh belonged here with him. And having them here was worth every ounce of worry and apprehension he'd suffered to get them here.

And the anxiety you continue to suffer, he thought, remembering the Kolheek Elder's odd parting words about seeing what fate had in store. Had he fallen in love with these children only to have them taken away from him in a mere two months? The idea was too disturbing for him to even contemplate, so he closed the lid on it, shut it out of his mind.

He climbed the stairs, and when he knocked softly on the closed door of their bedroom, the bumps and scuffling stopped. Travis turned the knob and stepped into the room.

His eyebrows raised when he saw that the blankets and quilted spreads of both twin beds were mangled and twisted. Jared stood on one mattress, towering over his brother Josh, the pillow in his grasp drawn back for a playful blow.

One look at Travis's face had Jared's grip on the pillowcase loosening. The pillow dropped to the mattress, bouncing once before coming to rest on top of the swirl of sheets and blankets. Jared slowly lowered himself until he was sitting next to his wide-eyed brother.

"Sorry," Jared muttered. "We was only playin'."

Scolding the boys hadn't even crossed his mind,

but the fear he read on little Josh's face made Travis wonder what kind of trouble their roughhouse games had gotten them into at the orphanage.

"I used to have pillow fights with my brother when we were kids." Travis went to Jared's empty bed and began to straighten the blankets.

"You did?" Realizing that Travis wasn't angry, Jared grinned like an imp.

"Yeah," Travis said. "It was a lot of fun." He turned down the top blanket and smoothed his hand over it. "But it's really late. You two need to get some sleep."

"But we ain't tired." Even as he said the words, Jared bounded off Josh's bed and onto his own, sliding down onto the mattress and tucking his feet under the covers.

"New situations have a way of getting you all worked up." Travis picked up the forgotten pillow from where it lay on Josh's bed, plumped it up and then tucked it behind Jared's head. "But if you'll lay still for a bit, I'm sure you'll fall asleep soon enough." Then he began to untangle Josh's bed-clothes.

Josh just stared at him. Finally the boy said, "It's quiet here."

Travis smiled as he drew the blanket up over Josh's legs. He had no idea what the child meant by the remark.

Then Jared spoke up. "At the home, Sammy cries. A lot. And Mrs. Basset turns up the TV really loud at night. She says we give her big pains 'cause she can't hear her shows. She gets pretty mad. Her face gets all red."

Realizing that the boys were explaining the difference between bedtime at the orphanage and here, Travis nodded. "I see."

"Mrs. Basset yells." Josh's voice was tiny. "Jared couldn't sleep with me. One boy to a bed. That's the rule."

The state home had housed at least two dozen other children. The twins were probably used to constant chaos, noise and mayhem. Living here would be a distinct contrast for them. It would take some getting used to, Travis silently surmised.

"You want Jared to sleep in your bed?"

Josh swallowed, blinked in anxious hesitation, then he nodded.

Travis looked over at Jared, lifted Josh's blanket and swiped his hand through the air in a movement meant to stir things into motion. "Don't worry," he told them softly. "You'll get used to the quiet. Silence can be a nice thing."

Jared scooted down onto the bed next to Josh. "B-but we ain't tired," he repeated his original complaint.

"We *aren't* tired." Travis couldn't help correcting the boy's improper grammar. "Like I said, if you lay still—"

"How about a story?"

Travis directed his gaze toward the soft, feminine voice coming from the doorway.

Diana was dressed in a simple white robe that was tied at the waist with a sash. Light glistened on the long, straight rope of hair that was pulled over one shoulder. The pristine fabric of the robe accentuated the coppery skin of her bare arms and legs.

Legs. Travis couldn't help but notice the shapely knees, firm calves and tiny ankles. Even her feet were cute.

The thought startled him and he felt his eyes go wide for a millisecond, before he forced his gaze back up to her face. Damn it! Ogling this woman's body was the last thing he'd meant to do!

He was human. A human male. The testosterone pumping though his veins made appreciating the female form a most inherent act. But if he was going to eye the woman every time they were in the same room together, he was going to be in for a long and uncomfortable couple of months.

"You—" His mouth and throat had gone dry at the sight of her and that made his voice sound gravelly. He shoved the awareness he felt aside, cleared his throat and started again. "You want to tell the boys a story?"

She nodded, her wide, sensuous mouth twisting wryly.

Her very kissable lips made his heart thud against his ribs.

"If I'm to get to sleep anytime soon," she quipped lightly, "I think Jared and Josh need a little spirit-calming medicine."

He cast her a quizzical glance. "Medicine?"

Her chuckle was velvety rich, like sweet cream, and the fine hairs on the back of his neck raised. Damn, but this woman was too...*appealing.*

Control yourself! he silently demanded.

"Don't worry," she said. "I'm not suggesting drugs. I'm talking about good, old-fashioned entertainment. Entertainment designed especially for..."

she then turned her attention first to Jared and then to Josh as she stole closer "…little boys at bedtime."

She sat down on the edge of Jared's bed. Travis was conscious of how close she was. He could smell the warm, clean, lemony fragrance of her.

"Long ago," she began, "before there were such things as paper and pencils, The People kept their history through stories. They sat around a fire at night with the stars winking at them high above, and they taught their children where they came from. They recounted tales of brave warriors and hunters. They told of times gone by. They told of their hopes and dreams to come. The children heard about floods and fire and acts of nature that formed the tribe into what it was. Through the Shaman's words, battles were relived. Wars with other tribes over hunting rights disputes. Wars with the Europeans. The children learned of the good times, when crops and hunting were bountiful. And they heard about hardships, when blizzards came, and stayed, and made hunting impossible. The Shaman would also tell of brave leaders and great chiefs…"

Travis looked at the faces of the twins, saw that Diana had caught them up in the web she was spinning. Easing himself down to sit on Josh's bed, Travis was extremely careful not to allow his knee to touch hers. She was so close. He looked at her face, at her expressive eyes, and found himself quickly pulled into the past right along with the boys. Her soft voice was lulling, mesmerizing, and he clearly understood what she meant when she'd said that storytelling was spirit-calming medicine.

"One such chief," she continued, "was called

Half Moon. He got his name from the pale, crescent-shaped scar he had here.'' She reached up and gingerly touched her face high on the left cheekbone. ''When he was a small child, he wandered into a pen of wild horses. His mother watched helplessly as the animals stampeded. They reared and bolted and bucked. They thrashed and finally broke the fence. Half Moon could have been killed. *Should* have been killed. But instead he walked from the pen all on his own. He'd been kicked in the face, the horse's hoof leaving a curved gash on his cheek. The whole tribe knew that Half Moon had survived what any normal child would not have. The People knew that Half Moon would be a great man when he grew. He would be smart. And brave. And he would lead The People toward wonderful things.''

Her words were like magic, drawing them deeper and deeper into the moment. Her eyes danced with emotion, her tone rose and then softened for the greatest impact. It was clearly evident that she'd told this tale many times. That she herself reveled in the history of her tribe. And that in this verbal tradition—whether the story was myth or reality—she was celebrating her proud heritage.

Travis tore his eyes from her beaming face and looked at the boys. They, too, were held entranced by the enchantment she conjured. This connection to the past *was* a good thing for Jared and Josh. Of that he couldn't be more sure than he was at this moment, seeing the fascination in their eyes.

''And Half Moon did grow to be a great man,'' Diana said. ''He was all the things The People knew he would be. He was a great chief. Wiser than many others. Half Moon was the man who made the Big Negotiation. He knew the Europeans were in our land to stay. He knew they would soon outnumber The People. So he made it possible for us to have a place. A home. He gathered his tribe and moved them to what is now known as Vermont. The Kolheek, People Of The Smoke—*your people*—survive today because Half Moon knew when to talk peace rather than engage in war.''

Pride seemed to emanate from her. Her spine was straight, her slender shoulders square. There was no conceit or arrogance in the way her chin tipped upward; however, there was a good measure of old-fashioned self-respect. And Travis couldn't help but admit that he found it alluring. *Highly alluring.*

Movement at the periphery of his vision had him darting a glance down the length of her body. Gravity tugged at the hem of her robe, parting the bottom facings to reveal a slice of her bronze-hued thigh. The sight of her finely honed muscle caused heat to curl in the bottom of his belly, his abdomen tensing with a sharp but pleasant pain. The sudden discomfort was a shock and the urge to suck in a lungful of air was overwhelming, but he successfully restrained it.

As inconspicuously as possible, he pressed his balled-up fist to his diaphragm, hoping to quell the constriction. Never before had he reacted to a woman in such a…a *physical* manner.

Women are trouble, a shadowy voice in his head warned.

Averting his gaze to the far corner of the room, he clenched his jaw. He didn't need any dark warnings.

He knew all about women. Knew the kind of wounds love inflicted. Had seen it in his parent's marriage. His brother's. Hell, he'd even experienced the pain firsthand back in college.

He wasn't interested in becoming trapped in any woman's web, no matter how beguiling it might seem.

He was just going to have to snuff out these feelings of attraction he felt for Diana. He could do it. Anytime—*every time*—he felt something even remotely resembling desire, he'd simply squash it. Like an irritating gnat.

Simple plans were the easiest to accomplish. And this plan couldn't be more simple. He could do it. She wasn't going to be here for long.

Apparently she'd finished her story. She was standing now, smiling at Jared and Josh. Then Diana turned that gorgeous smile on Travis, and it was as if he'd been struck between the eyes with a ball peen hammer.

"I'm going to say good-night," she told him.

Her voice flowed over him—through him—like the mellifluous notes of some haunting melody. Again, his gut tightened.

This is crazy, he told himself. *Damned crazy!*

"I'll leave you to tuck in the boys."

And then she was gone.

You can fight this. You're stronger than these idiotic feelings. Ignore this ridiculous attraction. Just ignore it.

But even as the thoughts marched drill-like through his brain, he unwittingly turned his head to inhale the faint, citrusy scent she'd left behind.

At last the house was quiet. Diana had brewed a pot of her own herb tea and was sitting in the all-season sunroom, looking out at the darkness, listening to the muffled quiet of the silent, wintry night. Pale moonlight cast a beautiful mélange of deep shadow and pearly glow among the thicket of pine and bare hardwood trees.

When she'd left Travis and his boys, Jared and Josh were both sleepy-eyed and ready for the sandman to take them on whatever dream adventure was in store for them this night. They were great kids, full of energy and imagination. They had delighted in the story she'd told of Half Moon, that much had been clear to Diana. But then, they were bright, inquisitive children. She knew she was going to enjoy spending time with them, aquainting them with their Kolheek heritage.

Travis had paid close attention to her story, too, Diana silently mused, lifting the mug to her lips and taking a small swallow of tea. Well, she hoped it was the legend that had held him so enthralled. His onyx eyes had latched onto her, making her feel as if he were staring into the very depths of her soul, and she'd had a hard time concentrating on the storytelling. She'd wanted to reach up and smooth her hair, fidget with the sash of her robe, but she'd forced her hands to remain in her lap. She hadn't liked feeling like a silly, squirming schoolgirl. Thank heaven she'd been able to quell the nervousness Travis's intent gaze had provoked in her. Soon, the training she'd received in the nearly lost art of storytelling had kicked in and she'd become engrossed in the past herself.

Still, when she thought about how his gaze had been riveted to her face, his attention focused on her every word… The memory caused shivers to careen down her spine like an icy mist, and she curled her hands around the heated ceramic mug to ward off the imagined chill. She tucked her bare feet under her on the padded seat of the wicker chair.

His interest had been in nothing more than the story, she firmly told herself. She refused to think anything else. He'd been captivated by Half Moon's experience. Anyone would be fascinated by the history of such a great chief's life.

But Travis's gaze was so dark, so… She couldn't quite put a name to what she saw in his eyes. Like secret windows. Seemingly filled with something deep and profound. Something mysterious. Haunting her. Calling to her.

Huffing out a frustrated sigh, she looked toward the ceiling. Why was she so intent on conjuring fantasies around this man? Her thoughts had seemed to have a mind of their own ever since she'd first laid eyes on Travis.

Head shaking slowly, she tried to clear her mind. She simply refused to allow her imagination to get the better of her.

But the thoughts persisted, refusing to be banished. What was it about him that provoked these sensuous notions running through her head? She'd had no trouble whatsoever deflecting the approaches made by other men since her divorce. She'd easily turned down all offers of dates, and she'd done so politely and tactfully so as not to hurt a single living soul. Yet here she was fancying that Travis Westcott—a man she barely knew—was staring at her…desiring her.

Desiring her? Is that where her thoughts were heading?

No. No. No. She couldn't have that. She wouldn't allow herself to be undermined by her own ridiculous imaginings. Travis had become caught up in her story. That was all—

"I'm glad to see you've made yourself at home."

She looked toward the French door that led into the house. His frame was backlit by the soft light being thrown from the kitchen. He looked strong. Safe. Protective.

Shaking her head slightly, she shoved the impressions from her, but not before she realized this wasn't the first time she'd been plagued by these same out-of-the-blue reflections. Ridding herself of the fanciful thoughts shouldn't be very difficult. Especially when she knew that *no* man would ever make her feel safe and protected.

"I'm in the habit of drinking some chamomile tea before bed," she told him, relieved that her voice sounded much less quivery than she felt inside. "So I made myself a pot."

His dark head bobbed slightly. "I hope you don't mind. I helped myself." He lifted the mug he held in his right hand. "May I join you?"

"Please."

This politeness, this formality, made her feel too awkward for words.

"Look, Travis, I'm awfully sorry that I've been foisted on you like this. I know you see me as an intruder in your home. Especially when, I'm sure, all you're thinking about is getting to know the boys, letting them get to know you and becoming a family so you can enjoy the Christmas holiday together.''

He didn't say anything at first, just sipped his tea, peering at her over the rim of the mug. Finally one of his shoulders lifted a fraction. ''This is what's best for the boys.''

She couldn't tell whether or not he believed what he said, but she was fascinated with those eyes of his. Even in the dim light of the porch, his gaze gleamed with some unnameable force, a humming energy she found mesmerizing.

The apology had been meant to somehow lessen the tenseness in the air. But all their small exchange seemed to accomplish was to make the oxygen denser, harder to breathe. She wanted to say something, to somehow break this awful silence, but it was as if the ability to speak had suddenly been lost to her.

''So—''

Not ready for the sound of his satiny voice, Diana actually started.

''—was it true? The story you told the boys?''

Nodding, she answered, ''Yes, the events I relayed to the boys really happened. Generations ago. Of course, I didn't go into too much detail. Jared and Josh are young. The simple version of the story is good enough for the time being.''

''The simple version?'' he asked. ''There's more?''

''Oh, yes. Much more.'' She shifted in the seat. ''Half Moon didn't come to the decision to negotiate with the Europeans easily. The Kolheek are proud and stubborn people. He fought first.''

"As well he should," Travis said. "The land he lived on belonged to him."

Diana slowly shook her head in modest dissent. "No one can really own the earth. But the right to hunt and live on the land was ours." She paused. "Well," she lightly amended with a tiny smile, "Half Moon believed the right belonged to The People."

Travis nodded, a new understanding—or was that interest?—lighting his eyes.

"Many men from the tribe, young and old, lost their lives in battle," she said, "before Half Moon decided to bargain with the Europeans. The wars went on for years. They were bloody. And relentless. It was an awful time in our history."

He sat with his feet planted apart, both hands grasping the mug of tea, his elbows resting on his knees. He was utterly silent, his gaze focused. *And he was staring directly at her mouth.*

Anxiety churned in her stomach at the realization. Was he hearing a word she said? It seemed as if he were in some sort of trance.

Ever so slowly, his tongue roved across his bottom lip. The action appeared utterly subliminal. As if he wasn't even aware of what he was doing. She didn't sense he was trying to flirt with her, but she did recognize that her worst fears were true. When she'd thought he might be feeling something for her, it hadn't just been her imagination. He *was* attracted to her. She was sure of that now.

Panic sent her thoughts into total commotion. She

should tell him this instant that she wasn't interested in any kind of association with him other than the purpose for her being here. Jared and Josh.

Just be honest with the man. Her grandmother's wise words echoed through her mind.

Diana opened her mouth to speak, but then the most extraordinary thing happened. Travis sat up straight. He looked out the window into the cold, snow-coated night. His chest rose and fell with a heaving, seemingly steeling breath. And when he directed his gaze at her again, there was not a single nuance of fascination or temptation or intimate interest expressed in his eyes. It was as if he'd extinguished his feelings like they were a candle flame that could easily be snuffed between a moistened index finger and thumb.

She felt her strained back muscles relax. Okay, so she now knew the truth. He *did* desire her. It wasn't her imagination. But it was also obvious that he intended to suppress his feelings, just as she meant to stifle hers.

The reason behind his decision didn't matter to her. She wasn't interested in what motivated him to mask his emotions. She was only glad he intended to control himself.

As long as they both contained the attraction they felt, everything would be just fine.

Chapter Three

"You brought home *who?*"

"She's a *what?*"

Travis suppressed a frustrated sigh as his medical partners and best friends, Greg and Sloan, asked their questions in unison. He'd known the men would be surprised by his news. But he hadn't expected this degree of astonishment.

"Look, guys," he said. "I can't go into too much detail. I have a patient due in at any moment."

"Oh, no." Sloan shook his head, catching Travis by the sleeve. "You aren't going anywhere until you explain."

His shoulders slumped in surrender as Travis turned back around. "I brought home a Medicine Woman from the reservation."

Greg snickered. Travis tossed him a narrow-eyed glare conveying a silent warning.

"So," Sloan said, "we did hear you correctly the first time."

Travis nodded.

Sloan's brow furrowed and he shook his head. "Why?"

"Well, the boys will be due for their..." The words caught in Travis's throat. He had no idea how his friends would react to what he was about to say.

In all the years he'd known Greg and Sloan, Travis's Native American heritage had never really been discussed. The opportunity for an earnest conversation about that fact had never arisen. Of course, they knew he was half-Kolheek; however, it had never been a subject that the three of them had ever delved into too deeply.

He'd become interested in his ancestry when he'd applied for college. The particular incident that had sparked his curiosity didn't make him very proud, but the important thing was that he'd finally become inquisitive about his Kolheek past.

For some reason, though, he'd more or less kept his interest to himself. Most peoples' family trees had roots in England, Ireland, China, Italy, or one or more of the dozens of other countries in the world. Just because the limbs and roots of his own family tree—half of it, at least—were buried deep in the soil of North America was no reason to go making a big deal of himself.

But he'd begun to read about his native tribe. Learned the Kolheek reservation was located in Vermont. He'd even made the effort to become a bona fide member of the Kolheek Nation by registering himself with the tribe. His mother hadn't been happy about his interest in his heritage. In fact, she'd been so upset by his actions that she'd disowned him altogether. It troubled him to think that she could feel such embarrassment by the same birthright he'd become so proud of. It also saddened him to know she wanted nothing to do with him because of his determination to explore his ancestry. However, it was really no great loss since his mother had always been more concerned with herself than she'd been with anyone else. So he hadn't let her opinions stop him. Once he began receiving the tribe's newsletter, he'd learned about Jared and Josh, orphans who needed heart surgery. Since then, his whole life had changed.

Still he hesitated in telling his friends the truth about Diana Chapman's presence in his home. He didn't like feeling anxious about being judged by his friends.

Looking down at the patient file he held in his hand, he ran his finger down along the stiff edge of the manila folder. Greg and Sloan had never judged him before. Why should they now?

"The boys are due for a naming ceremony about now," he told them, tipping up his chin to look them in the eye. "And because I know nothing of the heritage we share, I really can't prepare them the way Diana can. So she's going to teach them about the Kolheek culture. And then, when the boys are ready, she'll perform the ceremony. Give them their Indian names."

As he spoke, he noticed that the smirk that had been smeared across Greg's mouth slowly dissolved and then disappeared altogether. Both Greg and

Sloan sat up straighter, conveying clear and obvious interest in his explanation.

"Wow," Greg said, his voice soft. "That's great, Travis."

Sloan's head bobbed slowly, his eyes glittering with fascination. "The boys will get the chance to learn their heritage. I think that will be wonderful for them. Everyone needs to feel proud of who they are."

Relief washed over Travis. How could he ever have doubted these men? They were his best friends. The ones who stuck by him through thick and thin.

"It'll be perfect for the boys," Sloan continued. "And…for you."

Travis wasn't sure how to respond.

"Well, you are curious, aren't you?" Sloan asked. "About your heritage, I mean."

Shrugging, Travis had to admit, "Sure I am. I have been for years."

"We figured as much," Greg chimed in. "We know you're a compassionate person. We also figured you'd have helped the boys out with their medical problems no matter what their race. But it meant something to you. The fact that they're Native American…almost makes them…" He lifted one shoulder a fraction, then let it fall. "Family."

Becoming a father had changed Travis. He wasn't normally an emotional basket case. But as he looked from Sloan to Greg, his heart seemed to swell in his chest. It grew all achy. And unexpected moisture welled in his eyes, burning the backs of his lids.

He felt so lucky to have met these extraordinary men while the three of them had attended medical school together. And after discovering that, for one reason or another, they all lacked a close-knit family unit so essential to surviving the stresses of med school, they had decided to become—for each other—the support they didn't have. The three of them might not be blood brothers, but they were as close as three people could be. They laughed together. They cried together. They propped one another up when the chips were down.

Yes, Travis felt lucky, indeed.

His buddies had understood exactly how he felt, and he hadn't had to say a single word to explain his actions over the months that had turned into years since those sick little boys had first entered his life.

He sighed. "You guys..." Words lumped in his throat. He tried again, feeling the desperate need to let them know how he felt about them. About their friendship. "You guys..."

Sloan stopped him with an upraised palm. Greg's mouth quirked at the corners.

"Now don't go gettin' all mushy on us," Sloan said sternly.

"Yeah," Greg agreed, pushing his chair back, averting his gaze as he put unnecessary focus on rising to a stand. "Before we know it," he complained, his voice gruff, "we'll all be crying like a bunch of big babies. We can't have that. All of us have patients to see."

Travis just stood there looking at them.

So. Words weren't needed. Still, he was glad they knew how he felt.

Friends. There was nothing else like them in the whole wide world.

Shaking his head, Travis offered them a small smile, and then he went off to do his job.

The tingle of awareness Diana felt over every inch of her skin alerted her that Travis had entered the kitchen. Before meeting him, she'd never before experienced this prickly sensation. It was silly, she knew. She'd been a married woman not all that long ago. She knew all she wanted to know about men, women and their relationships. But still, every time she was near Travis, she became engulfed by this delicious giddiness that had her wanting to grin like a senseless child. However, simpering like an idiot didn't fit in with the professional image she was trying to project to him—so she strangled the urge with imaginary hands.

"Hi," he greeted.

The sonorous timbre of his voice made her flush with heat. She nodded a hello and then reached up to smooth her fingertips over her lips and chin. The action might have looked inconsequential, but it helped her to keep her smile in check. It wouldn't do for him to discover just how happy it made her merely to see him.

"How did it go at the school?" she asked.

After work, Travis had gone to register the boys for kindergarten at the local public school.

"Pretty good." He set his attaché case on the table beside her notepad and began to unbutton his overcoat. "I met the boys' teacher. Her name is Mrs. Brown. She seems nice."

"Good. What did she have to say about the…situation?"

He pulled off his coat and tossed it over the back of the nearest kitchen chair. "She made a great suggestion."

Interest had Diana's eyebrows raising, her silence encouraging him to elaborate.

"Mrs. Brown thought, with all the new things the boys are already trying to become accustomed to, me, their new home, you, and learning something about their culture…well, she felt that the boys should just take a couple of weeks at home. School will break for the Christmas holidays soon. And Mrs. Brown felt it would be good to have the boys start school when all the other kids come back at the beginning of the new year."

Diana nodded. "So they can take this new life of theirs in stages." She pulled her hand from her face, her smile broadening. "Sounds like Mrs. Brown is a smart woman."

He chuckled. "I think so, too. I don't mind having a little extra time with the boys. I've already worked on getting my schedule lightened up so I can spend more time with them."

Glancing toward the doorway, he frowned. Then his dark eyes once again found hers.

"They seem skittish," he said. "Like they think I'm going to take them back to the orphanage, or something."

"That's pretty normal, I would think," Diana said, wanting to assuage the worry that clouded his gaze. "They've voiced some fears to me. Nothing that a little time and trust won't cure." Then she assured him, "I let them know they can trust you as often as I can."

That prickly sense skated across every inch of her skin when she saw gratitude soften his features.

"Thank you. Very much."

His tone was like warm honey, golden and sensuously sweet, and Diana had to fight the urge to close her eyes and get lost in it.

"Oh, I nearly forgot." He reached for his briefcase, opened it and extracted several sheets of paper. "Mrs. Brown wants to know if the boys know their numbers and letters—"

"Sure thing." Diana reached for the papers. But when he didn't release them, she lifted a questioning gaze to his.

Awkwardness coated his face like a sheen of perspiration.

"I wasn't giving out orders," he told her gently. "I didn't mean that this was something you should do."

"Oh." Automatically she tucked her bottom lip between her teeth. She let her fingers slide from the sheets, her hand dropping to the tabletop. "It sure wasn't my intention to step on your toes. I only meant to offer to help..."

Clearly they were both discomfited by the moment. The air turned stiff. Thick. And she got the distinct sense that this awkwardness had nothing whatsoever to do with the papers he'd brought home from the school.

Finally he said, "Look, we need to relax. Every time we're around each other we seem to get all...bent out of shape."

Relax. The suggestion was a good one, but for some reason Diana couldn't see it happening.

Awareness scampered over her nerve endings whenever he was anywhere near her. She might be able to suppress her reaction to Travis—and she was sure determined to hide what she felt—but to really and truly relax? That just wasn't going to happen.

Travis cast another glance toward the living room where Jared and Josh were sitting in front of the television. "They're busy watching that Robin Hood video, so I think I'll start some dinner."

"Let me finish my notes," she told him, "and then I'll give you a hand."

He went to the pantry and pulled open the door. "What are you writing? Something about the boys?" He pulled out several potatoes and an onion and carried them to the counter.

"Yes. Actually I am." She picked up the pen that lay on the tabletop. "They fascinate me." She knew her eyes glittered with her memories of the day spent with Josh and Jared. But she couldn't help it. Not having spent much time with children in the past, she hadn't really been sure what to expect. She'd enjoyed herself, and she'd discovered that she liked the boys. Very much. "They're twins. They look so much alike. But they're as different as night and day."

Travis stood at the counter peeling the vegetables. He smiled. "They are, aren't they?"

"We bundled up this morning," she continued, "and took a long walk out back in the woods. I asked them to point out as many living things as they could. Jared ran and jumped and rolled." Diana chuckled as she remembered the child's antics. "But Josh mostly stayed by my side. Quiet. Contemplative."

"There's a good reason for that, I think." He put down the paring knife, turned to face her, leaning his hip against the edge of the counter. "The boys developed heart defects very early. Josh was much sicker than Jared. He ended up needing several operations. The poor kid wasn't allowed out of bed for months while he was recuperating. He's much less physically active than his brother."

Curiosity got the better of her. Curling her fingers around the pen, she tucked her fist under her chin and quietly said, "I heard that you were the one who made the operations possible. Tell me…what moved you to help them?"

One of his muscular shoulders lifted in a small shrug, as if he wanted to cast aside the importance of what he'd done. He returned to the task of peeling the potatoes.

"I don't know," he said. But he was quick to continue. "I was still working my residency. I'd just received confirmation of my membership into the tribe. And that very week the first tribal newsletter showed up in my mailbox." His hands paused and he glanced toward the ceiling as if contemplating some deep, philosophical notion. When he looked at her, his coal-black eyes were intense.

"Do you believe in fate?" he asked. Then he chuckled. "Maybe I'm just being silly." Again, he shrugged. "But I couldn't get those boys and their problem out of my mind. The article I read said the state and the reservation were feuding over who should pay for the twins' medical needs. I had to step forward and do what I could. I had to. Time was running out for those boys."

"So you contacted the hospital?" Diana said.

"Uh-huh. And I harassed and badgered my fellow residents, the teaching doctors, and anyone else who would listen until a heart surgeon stepped forward." Travis laughed. "I think Doctor Harris agreed to operate on the boys simply to shut me up. He did all the necessary procedures—and they turned out to be substantial—at no cost to the state or the reservation. He's a good man."

"So are you, Travis. So are you."

Had it really been her mouth, her tongue, that had formed the whispery, awe-filled opinion? An opinion regarding a near stranger she'd only just met a couple of days ago?

Diana hadn't moved from her spot at the table. There had to have been at least eight feet separating the two of them, yet when he turned his raven gaze on her, she felt as if he was but a hair's breath away.

Her mind whirled, her thoughts an incomprehensible jumble. Her heart pounded so hard that all she heard was its *thud, thud, thud,* deep in her chest. The oxygen in the room seemed to jell into some kind of glutinous mass she couldn't have pulled into her lungs if her life depended on it. And, unfortunately, it did.

He seemed as frozen as she as he stood there with the paring knife poised but forgotten against the half-peeled potato. His jet-black eyes sparked and flashed with…with…

The ink pen slid from her fingers, clattering and bouncing on the wooden top of the kitchen table. The noise acted like a hypnotist's snapping fingers, abruptly bringing them back to the present, saving them from whatever stupor had been threatening the both of them.

Embarrassment suffused her face with heat, but thankfully, Travis quickly returned to his task, his gaze no longer fastened to hers.

Had she gone totally insane? she wondered frantically. What had possessed her to utter such a startling—such a *revealing*—postulate?

Lord, above! Had those words really been uttered as throatily and sensuously as they had sounded to her own ears? She was mortified.

What must he be thinking? And how could she fix this? How could she mend the moment? Should she make light of her comment? No, that would only demean his heroic behavior where the boys were concerned.

There is no fixing this, the small voice of common sense told her. *Change the subject,* it continued to press. *Pretend the words never left your mouth, and shove this whole situation into high gear. Move forward. Tap into another conversation…*any *conversation.*

"So—"

Even though his tone was quiet, Diana hadn't anticipated it and her head jerked up in sudden reaction.

"—did the boys pass your test?"

"Test?" She blinked at his profile, feeling foolish that she didn't understand his question.

"In the woods today," he said. "You said you asked them to point out living things."

"Oh, right." Absently she plucked up the pen from where it had landed and fingered it nervously. "It wasn't a test, really," she told him. "I—I was…trying to relay…to the boys, of course…that all living things are…well, that they're sacred. That we should respect…a-and…''

Her vocabulary seemed to have dissipated into thin air. She couldn't put four words together without losing her grip on the rest of the sentence.

She swallowed. Took a deep breath.

Endeavoring to continue, she said, ''We had a great d-discussion about the trees. Jared argued… well, he thought the trees weren't alive. Because they had lost their leaves. They looked as if they had died.'' The chuckle she emitted sounded awkwardly forced even to her own ears.

Oh, my, she thought, looking down at her notepad, *I'm only making this worse.* Why had the discussion with the boys seemed so poignant, so important, when she had been in the park with them? The subject sounded downright silly now.

Her gaze darted to where Travis stood. Why did the man's shoulders have to be so broad? Why did he have to roll his shirtsleeves up to reveal his sinewy forearms? Why did that delighted sparkle in his black-as-midnight gaze have to make her heart trip in her chest like a boulder rolling, careering down a mountain, wild, uncontrollable, dangerous?

''But Jared figured it out,'' she forced herself to finish, ''that the trees had to be alive…you see… since they grow new leaves every spring.''

She noticed her hand trembling, felt her blood rushing through her body. This was crazy! Abruptly she stood, the legs of the chair grating against the floor.

Their gazes locked, and it was then that Diana saw it. In those keenly discerning eyes of his.

He knew! He perceived the chaos she was experiencing. So much for hiding how appealing she found him.

He knew something else, too. She sensed it. Realized it down to the marrow of her bones. He knew that *she* knew that the both of them had been momentarily mesmerized…and that she was now striving to cover that fact, and failing miserably at the attempt.

"You know," she blurted, "I've come down with an awful headache. I think I'll go lay down. Don't wait dinner on me. I'm not that hungry."

Without giving him a single second to utter a word, she raced from the room.

Raw desire. That's what had been expressed in Travis's intense gaze. His need had been as clear as the light of day.

She'd never in her life seen eyes as black. She'd never in her life seen such fierce hunger. Such concentrated intensity.

Diana pressed her back against the closed door of the guest bedroom where she was staying, leaning into it with all her weight as if she meant to keep the whole world at bay. No, not the whole world. Only Travis. And the passion he'd so blatantly exuded.

He moved her. Affected her. She had realized it from the beginning. Almost from the very moment she'd met him.

She'd vowed to suppress the attraction. Extinguish it completely. But it kept rekindling itself, like the embers of some smoldering fire that were fanned and brought back to blazing life by his very presence.

And she'd been certain that he, too, had meant to crush any visceral urges he might have. She'd witnessed his determination to suppress the attraction he felt the very first night she'd spent in his home. She was sure of it.

Yet there they had stood in the kitchen, gawking at each other like teens, ripe, randy and nearly panting.

Well, she wasn't a randy teen. She was a grown woman. And she refused to allow herself to even think about having any kind of physical relationship with Travis Westcott.

What she was feeling was only a whim. A whim that could be conquered. That *would* be suppressed.

Closing her eyes, she whispered a silent prayer that these ridiculous feelings could be vanquished. Completely subjugated. Because if they couldn't, she'd surely be humiliated beyond words.

Chapter Four

The winter moon hung fat and round in a black satin sky, its glow casting long shadows across the kitchen floor. Shadows that Travis barely saw as he sat at the table in deep contemplation. It was after eleven, and he was certain that hunger or thirst would soon drive Diana from her room where she'd hidden since before dinner.

Hours ago, he'd tucked the boys into bed. He'd showered. Spent some time studying a few patient files. And then he'd tried to sleep. But he'd tossed and turned, his blankets ending up a tangled mess around his knees.

He'd attempted to focus his thoughts on Diana's afternoon with the boys. Josh and Jared had been full of tales during dinner, and again at their bath time. Apparently Diana had once more woven her Medicine Woman magic on the twins.

One tale was about an ancient tree, wise, patient

and steadfast, that had been satisfied to spend its entire life sheltering wildlife and shading humans who came to stand under its branches. Another story related the Indian's deep regard for woodland birds and how important it was to be able to identify the song of each species. A smart hunter would learn to decipher the warning calls of birds, so one would be alerted to intruders.

Quiet Josh even told Travis how Diana had said that the earth itself is alive and constantly changing. The boy had sat in the tub filled with bubbles, his eyes wide with awe.

Travis had to agree. He'd told Josh that the earth was always becoming different through earthquakes and volcanoes and erosion caused by both wind and rain, the elements of nature.

"Diana says," Jared had piped up, "that we should be really careful of every living thing. Wiggly caterpillars, all the birds, the bears, the trees and flowers and bushes. Everything."

Josh's nose had wrinkled as he'd added, "Even creepy spiders."

Diana's lesson today was making his boys think, Travis realized. The simple walk she'd taken with them through the woods had turned into a way for her to help develop the boys' consciences. The Native American philosophy, nurturing a healthy respect for life, was a great idea. Travis couldn't help but feel this very thing was missing in the upbringing of many children today. Why else was there such violence among teens and young adults? Why else did people care so little about the polluting of rivers, lakes and land with their "throwaway" mentality?

Diana had affected his boys in a very profound way today, and he'd made a mental note to express his appreciation to her.

As he'd lain alone in his bed, he'd begun to ponder, for the umpteenth time, his sorely lacking knowledge of his Kolheek heritage. He had questions. So many questions. He was sure Diana wouldn't mind answering them. However, over the past three days that she'd been here, he hadn't been able to work up the courage to ask.

Since he'd arrived home from the reservation, Travis's whole world had changed. Yes, he was a father now. And, of course, that fact alone was enough to disrupt anyone's existence. But the change he had noted included more than just his new status as a parent. He had to admit it.

Travis felt as if his home had been invaded by some gorgeous, ethereal goddess.

Confident in his thoughts and opinions, he'd always seen himself as a man who was happy and content. Satisfied with who he was. Yet, his confidence seemed to wither away to nothing when Diana was anywhere within sight.

He continued to be astonished by the regal serenity that appeared to permeate her being. Her rich brown eyes seemed so darned...all-knowing. And her voice—

It had been the memory of that voice—the sensuous echoes still ringing in his head from when she'd expressed her opinion of him being a good person—that had chased him out of his bed and down into the darkness of the kitchen.

He wanted Diana. Wanted to kiss her. Touch her.

Run his fingers through her long, silken hair. He wanted to press his nose to her neck. Smell what he knew would be the delicate lemon scent of her sun-kissed skin.

Damn! He had to stop this. He had to stop it *now*.

But quelling the hungry thoughts wasn't going to be easy. Because he'd learned something this evening. He'd learned that Diana, too, suffered with the same wild attraction as he. The desire she'd felt had been clearly evident. Her dark gaze had sparked with it. Her voice had reflected it. Her whole body had grown quivery with it.

Even she had been shocked by the sensuousness of her tone. By the raw eroticism lacing the words that had tumbled from her oh-so-luscious lips. In fact, she'd been so aghast at herself that she'd barely been able to tell him about her afternoon with the boys. And then she had run. She had pleaded a headache and imprisoned herself upstairs.

He knew she had probably hoped to somehow erase the moment. That the old adage 'out of sight, out of mind' might ring true. But it didn't. No matter that she had locked herself away from him, Travis couldn't get her words—or her ardent tone—out of his head.

Well, Travis decided as he sat waiting for her, this had to be discussed. He had to tell Diana that he had no intention of acting on his feelings.

No matter how much his body might want to.

And he didn't even have a problem with telling her why. If he laid it all out on the line, if he clarified his thoughts, explained his past, rationalized his motives, surely she'd understand and the two of them could brush this attraction thing under the rug.

Movement at the kitchen doorway caught his eye.

"I'm sorry—"

She was backing away even before she'd entered the room.

"—I thought you'd be in bed."

"Diana," he softly beckoned. "Come back. We need to talk."

"Something wrong with the boys?"

He couldn't see alarm on her face, the dusky shadows prevented that, but he did hear it in her voice. And her concern for the twins touched him deep inside, squeezing at his heart like a C clamp.

Why was he so stirred by this woman?

"No," he told her softly. "They're fine. This has to do with you and me. Just…you and me."

"C-could it wait?" she asked, obvious nervousness giving her voice a breathy quality. "I only came down for a drink. And to rummage around for a cracker or two."

"You missed dinner. Would you like a sandwich? Or I could heat up some of the leftovers for you."

"No, thank you."

Trepidation fairly pulsed from her. He understood fully how she was feeling. This wasn't a topic he relished delving into, either. However, he couldn't let this go another day. It had to be discussed. Put behind them. For good.

She still hadn't left the threshold of the kitchen door.

"Sit." The single word was quietly spoken, but it

sounded just like what it was, a command. Reaching over, he pulled out a chair for her.

Silence seemed to reign supreme in the darkness for several momentous seconds. At last, she expelled a small surrendering sigh, and then she crossed the floor, lowered herself into the chair.

Moonlight shone in her dark eyes, gleamed on her hair, bringing to mind a river of shimmering blackness. And if Travis had thought her attractive before this moment, he couldn't help but note how the night, the shadows, the moon glow only heightened her beauty. Heat twisted in his gut.

Silently cursing, he did what he could to stamp out the fever she kindled in him.

"Look, Diana—"

He hadn't meant to begin so gruffly. This was a subject that needed to be broached delicately. Otherwise, he risked embarrassing her. And himself, too. That wasn't his intention. For either of them.

After taking a deep breath and moistening his lips, he began again, "We need to discuss this..."

His speech trailed.

This...*what?* he wondered frantically. What should he call this huge thing that sparked and sizzled between them?

A need?

A hankering?

He cleared his throat. Looked toward the ceiling. Then leveled his gaze on her once again.

"I've been feeling—" His teeth clamped down on his top lip. "Ever since we first met, I've found you—"

Words failed him, again and again. He turned his

face from her, pondering the brass cabinet knobs reflecting the moonbeams. Why couldn't he express his thoughts? What was it that was holding him back?

He had no doubt at all about what he was feeling himself, but was he sure of what he suspected Diana was feeling? Mentally he shook his head. He didn't simply suspect. He was positive. Absolutely sure.

"What you need to know," he blurted out, "is that I'm not interested in a relationship. I know in my heart that men and women can't get along for any length of time. My parents brutalized each other during their divorce. My brother and his wife did, too. In fact, my brother has been running from the pain so hard and so fast that he can't stay in one place long enough to establish a residence or leave a forwarding address. I won't allow that kind of pain into my life. I just won't. So…whatever it is that gets us all shaken up when we're in the same room…well…we need to just cool it…back off and…and control ourselves."

Her knee-jerk reaction to his assertive soliloquy brought to mind a tiny, defenseless animal that had been backed into a corner. Panic etched itself on her face. And she looked as if she had no place to run. No place to hide.

Then her cinnamon eyes narrowed with a fluffed up irritation as she made an attempt at anger. Anger meant to cover the truth.

But Travis wasn't fooled. Not in the least.

If he hadn't felt so threatened by the subject himself, he just might have smiled at her performance. Most anyone, when confronted so blatantly, would have gone on the attack. Most anyone would have lashed out, called him names, deemed him arrogant and big-headed and presumptuous.

But not Diana. She might want to, but she wouldn't. Her quiet dignity wouldn't allow her to let her ire fly.

Funny how Travis was so sure of that fact. He felt he knew her that well, even though he'd just met her a few days earlier.

Slowly, but purposefully, she stood. "I don't want to talk about this."

He stood, too, as he said, "We might not want to discuss it, but we must. I'm just glad you're not going to deny it."

One perfectly arched eyebrow lifted just a fraction. "What if I did?"

"I'd have to call you a liar," he told her quietly. "And that would mortify you. If nothing else, Diana, you're honest to the bone. You said so yourself, a person is only as good as his or her character."

They faced off in the moonlight. He, determined to make her admit what was happening between them, she, seemingly just as determined to refuse to discuss the issue.

Finally he softly said, "If you did try to dispute me, I'd have to prove my point."

He reached out for her at the same instant her brow wrinkled with a tiny frown.

"Don't." Her plaintive whisper was barely audible.

But it was too late.

He'd already touched her. Already felt her in his arms, her breasts pressing against his chest. Already smelled the light citrus scent of her skin wafting around him. Already experienced the heat of her flesh through the thin satin robe.

This was crazy! his brain shouted. But that's how he felt whenever he was near her. Over-the-edge crazy.

Don't kiss her! Don't you dare kiss her!

The thoughts were strong. Insistent. Demanding. But his want, his need was stronger. More insistent. More demanding.

Her gaze was mere inches from his. He could feel her warm breath brush against his cheek.

Her panic quickly subsided, as did his own. What replaced it was a desire so damned raw it hurt, so damned exposed that neither of them could possibly dispute it.

The next instant her mouth was crushed beneath his in a kiss that could only be described as frantic. Hot and wet and wild.

He let his tongue lightly graze her bottom lip, the smooth silken heat of it pushing him further into the pure and perfect pleasure of his passionate insanity. She parted her lips, her tongue shyly connecting with his.

The groan he emitted came from down deep in his throat. The sound of it nearly overpowered her tiny, breathy gasp.

He hadn't realized it before this moment, but she'd woven her fingers into his hair and she was tugging him closer, closer. With both hands. He cradled her face in his palms. Then his fingertips slid back further to explore the outer edges of her ears, the delicate length of her throat, the curve of her shoulder.

The both of them were well and truly swept away.

One of her hands flattened against his chest, and then he felt the fabric of his T-shirt tighten as she slowly clenched it in her fist.

His heart pounded furiously, hot blood raging through his body.

More. More. The madness ate away at his mind. Rational thought was nowhere to be found.

Her robe parted beneath his touch, and suddenly his skin felt aflame as he cupped the roundness of her breasts in his palms.

The intimate contact made their eyes fly open at the same instant, and he eased away as if he'd been blistered by the heat of her. He took a backward step at the same instant she did. She tugged her robe into place, straightened her hair, her fingers feathering over her mouth, neither of them able to take their eyes off the other.

She swallowed, and Travis felt a deep disappointment at not having had the opportunity to press his lips against the long length of her elegant neck, or nip at her tender earlobes, or nibble on the line of her jaw.

Closing his eyes, he took a moment to inhale deeply. To try to gather his wits. Garner his strength. Rein in the need throbbing through him like the heavy beat of an insistent drum.

Unwittingly he reached up and combed agitated fingers through his hair. Then he stuffed his hands deep into the pockets of his trousers as he forced himself to look into her wide, dark eyes.

Her shoulders straightened, as did her spine, as she slipped back into some semblance of her pride as easily as if it had been the white satin robe she wore.

"Well," she said, her tone husky and sexy as hell, "I guess you're right. There really is no renouncing it."

Strange, he thought. She, too, had obviously been unable to come up with a word to describe the fever from which they both suffered.

It, she'd said.

That would have to do, he thought. If they were lucky, they'd never have to put a name to it. They could acknowledge its presence, yet refuse it power over them.

If they were lucky.

"Like you," she continued, "I'm not interested in a relationship. Of *any* kind. Serious. Frivolous. Physical. Whatever. I'm just plain not interested. In fact, I'll do everything in my power to avoid becoming involved. With you, or anyone else for that matter."

His eyes widened a fraction at the surprising resolve he heard in her tone. But he quickly nodded in the dark. "Good." Again he nodded. "I'm glad we agree."

"Oh, yes. We definitely agree."

His head continued to bob. As if its up and down motion somehow lent more credence to their decision.

The silence grew awkward.

He said, "Okay, then. We're in agreement about this."

She said nothing. But he knew their thoughts were unified.

"Then I'll go on up to bed." He moved past her, taking care not to touch her. "And let you get yourself a little something to eat."

But as he walked out of the kitchen and down the hall toward the stairs that would take him to his room, something nagged at him like the irritation of a poking stick.

Travis had explained the motives behind his decision not to become involved with Diana. Well…maybe not all of them. But his parents' divorce, and his brother's, too, were powerful reasons for him not to want the entanglements of a relationship. However, Diana had only expressed her aversion to relationships. And a stern aversion it had been, too.

As he climbed the stairs, a question whispered across his brain.

What had caused such hardness in her?

Saying that the restaurant wasn't much to look at from the outside was an understatement. It was a dive. A hole in the wall. But it was clean and off the beaten path, so the majority of the diners were urban residents rather than Christmas tourists seeking fancy city lights and holiday shopping that Philadelphia had to offer. Besides that, the cook had nearly fifty years of experience. The good food and the battle stories were what brought Travis, Sloan and Greg to the place for lunch at least twice a week.

"Would the two of you just grow up," Sloan said. "Travis, you're a big boy. You ought to be able to control your hormones. And, Greg, stop baiting the poor man."

Sloan indicated Travis with a jerk of his head.

"But you heard what he said," Greg complained. "The woman is driving him crazy. I'm just suggesting that he quit fighting it and dive headfirst into sexual dementia.''

''Now, there's a new disorder for the psychology journals,'' Sloan murmured with a chuckle. ''Keep this up, Greg, and you'll make into the annals of medical history, yet.''

Greg's head bobbed, his face plastered with pride. ''I'm working on it.''

''I shouldn't have said anything.'' Travis glanced off toward the far corner of the room. These men might be his best friends, as well as his business partners, but sometimes their good-natured ribbing could rub a man the wrong way. He sunk his chin down onto his fist as he turned back to them, murmuring softly, ''But Diana really is driving me nuts.''

''The two of you have talked about this…this…'' Sloan paused, then continued, ''About what's going on between you?''

''Only to the point of agreeing that it's not something we want to get involved in,'' Travis told him.

''Well, why don't you just take my advice?'' Greg's palms lifted upward. ''Why don't you just engage in one, good make out session?''

Of course, Greg would hand out that advice, Travis silently surmised. The man was in love. He'd found the woman of his dreams. In fact, he was going to marry Jane Dale on Christmas Eve.

Greg continued, ''You know, even a single kiss might get the whole thing out of your system.''

''Tried that,'' Travis said. ''Last week. Nearly melted the darned soles off my shoes.''

Of course, when he and Diana had shared that hotter-than-the-sun's-surface kiss he hadn't been wearing any shoes. But the phrase got his idea across. That's all that was necessary.

"You kissed the woman?" Greg's green eyes sparkled with interest. "Why didn't you tell us?"

Sloan frowned and gave Greg a nudge with his elbow. "What's wrong with you? He's not one to kiss and tell." He shook his head, his expression twisting with what could only be described as mild censure. "You're acting like a gossipy woman."

Greg's whole face scrunched up at what he obviously took as horrendous criticism. "Men don't gossip."

Sloan and Travis shared a sidelong glance. Finally Travis couldn't stop the grin tugging at the corners of his mouth. Sloan broke out in a snicker.

Greg only glowered at them.

"Maybe you should try talking to her about it again," Sloan suggested to Travis.

"No way." Travis shook his head adamantly. "I don't dare bring it up again. I can't." A sigh burst from deep in his chest. "But I can tell you that every time I'm even near the woman, I feel like I'm going to climb right out of my skin."

Every look, every word they exchanged since their late-night kiss seemed charged with some kind of heated current. A couple of times over the past week they'd accidentally touched, once when they'd cleaned up the dinner dishes together, another time when she'd backed into him, not knowing he was behind her, and each time he'd thought his heart was going to go into fibrillation. His pulse would go all erratic, and blood would whoosh through his ears. He was turning into a complete and total wreck.

Travis was disgusted with himself. He refused to allow his truant testosterone to get the better of him.

Just then, Greg's fiancée, Jane Dale, entered the restaurant and approached the table.

"Hey, guys," she called cheerily.

She leaned over and gave Greg a full-on-the-mouth kiss. Immediately, Travis was reminded of Diana...of the kiss they had shared...of his desire to kiss her again...

"Just stopped by to say hi," Jane said.

"Want something to eat?" Greg asked her.

"No, thanks," she said. "I have a thousand errands to run. And some shopping to do, too."

"How did the fitting go?" Greg asked Jane.

Jane's smile brightened up the whole room. "The dress is going to be beautiful. And the seamstress making the alterations is doing a fabulous job. Quick, too."

Travis just smiled, hiding his true thoughts. Greg and Jane were getting married in four short days. They had only met last month. Travis wanted to warn Greg that he was in for some heartache. Two people just couldn't stay together without hurting each other. Sure, Greg and Jane might be happy now. But give them a few months—a few years, if they were lucky. Then the hurting would begin. It always did. Eventually.

But he knew his friend wouldn't listen. Greg was drowning in the sentimental, lovesick emotions he felt for Jane. The poor guy was just going to have to learn the hard way.

"Travis," Jane said, attracting his attention and his gaze, "Greg told me about Diana. A Medicine Woman? That's fabulous for the boys."

Nodding and smiling, Travis couldn't help but feel Diana's presence in Philadelphia was a double-edged sword. She was wonderful for the boys. But she was hell on him.

"I'm sorry I've been so busy getting things ready for this wedding," she said. "I've wanted to come meet the twins. But you'll bring them to the wedding, right? Oh, and Diana, too." Jane's smile widened. "She can be your date."

"Great!" Travis's eyes rolled heavenward. "Just what I need. A date with the very woman I've been trying to avoid." He got up and tossed some money on the table to pay for his sandwich. "I'll meet you guys back at the office."

"What?" Jane looked from Greg to Sloan and back again. "What did I say?"

"Nothing, honey," Greg told her. "The poor man's just having some hormone problems."

"You're sick?" Jane asked.

Travis heard honest concern in her question, but he didn't turn back around. He simply continued toward the door knowing full well that Sloan and Greg wouldn't miss the opportunity to clear up the matter for her and in doing so make him the object of some joke or other that they would think hilarious. Sure enough, his friends didn't disappoint him.

"He's sick, all right." Greg cast forth a boisterous laugh.

"Yeah," Sloan chimed in. "He's suffering from sexual dementia."

Travis only groaned under his breath, his face flaming red, as he shoved his way out the door and onto the sidewalk. Hormone problems? Sexual dementia? Had his friends completely lost their minds?

He wanted to deny it. Vehemently. But he couldn't. He was afraid his friends were as sane as could be. He was also afraid they had correctly diagnosed his situation.

Chapter Five

Diana felt a little like an outsider at the small wedding reception. It was clear that Travis held Greg and Sloan in great esteem. The three men were more like brothers than friends. They razzed one another, hugged one another often during this special occasion and laughed with each other frequently, just as family is wont to do.

Jane, the new Mrs. Greg Hamilton, was gorgeous in her full-skirted white wedding gown. Her honey-blond hair was upswept in an elegant French twist and her short, pearl-studded veil floated around the back of her head like a tiny tulle cloud.

When Travis had explained that Jane had planned the wedding in less than a month, Diana could hardly believe it. However, with the way the bride's blue-gray eyes danced with joy, not to mention the fact that she and her new husband touched and kissed at every opportunity, it was clear that Jane and Greg had fallen for each other hard and fast, whatever the circumstances of their short courtship. The two of them were deeply in love.

Diana only hoped that their wedded bliss lasted longer than her own had.

Bliss? Had she ever experienced overwhelming happiness while she'd been married to Eric? Even on the day they had exchanged vows?

Looking at the rapture Jane was so obviously feeling, Diana came up feeling empty inside.

No, she and her ex had never encountered anything resembling the kind of wedded bliss that Greg and Jane were feeling. Diana was certain.

The mere thought of the months she'd spent as a married woman made her chest fill with emotions that were dark and thick and viscous. Sometimes the recollections—and the self-blame—became so strong, they swirled and rolled around her, catching her up and tossing her to and fro as if they were mighty hurricane winds. This time, she successfully pushed her way out of the memories before they could take hold of her and pull her into their sordid and ugly vortex.

At that moment, Diana watched as Greg and Jane danced together, both of them holding close a red-headed toddler that Travis had said was Greg's baby daughter, Joy. The three of them made such a sweet family. Diana offered up a quick and silent prayer for the Hamiltons' happiness.

Glancing around the small banquet hall, Diana again felt an acute twinge of being out of place here. She'd protested when Travis had asked her to attend the marriage celebration. The last place she needed to be was in a confined room with Travis dressed to the nines in that dark tuxedo and crisp white shirt. The midnight-black jacket matched his eyes to a T, his long, straight hair was tied back in a neat queue. Shivers coursed over every inch of her skin as unbidden images invaded her mind…images of what it would be like to have his long, satiny hair loose and brushing against her naked flesh. Her eyes went wide at the startling vision, and she forced herself to look away from him.

Ever since that night in the kitchen, when they had shared that soul-wrenching kiss, Diana had become more aware of him than ever. If that were possible. And Diana had quickly discovered it was.

His every word, his every move, intruded on her senses, encroached on her day-to-day activities, violated her dreams. It was getting to the point that, when they were together, thought rushed out of her head, the words in her mind turning to smoke she couldn't quite grasp.

She hated to lay down at night to sleep, for images of his face, his lips, his hands, his body, would torment her in disjointed, erotic apparitions. Every time she closed her eyes, her subconscious conjured Travis as some sort of nocturnal specter who teased her with kind words, taunted her with his warm, silken fingertips. Sleep had become agony for her.

So when he'd suggested she come to the wedding, she'd declined. But he'd been so full of rationale meant to convince her to change her answer. This gathering would be a great opportunity for Diana to meet his friends, he'd said, the people who would be close to the boys as they grew into adolescents and then adults. Besides that, he'd continued, the twins might have some questions regarding Native American marriage customs that he wouldn't be able to answer.

Diana had silently but seriously doubted that. The boys were too young to think about such things; however, in the end she'd agreed to come, thinking that any opportunity to talk to them about their heritage would be good. And she *had* been curious about Travis's friends and their children.

She smiled now as she spied Jared and Josh being herded around the room by Sloan's triplets, the girls introducing the boys to various people in attendance. Travis's sons would surely flourish in this friendly and loving environment.

"You're sitting over here all alone."

Travis's unexpected appearance made her flinch.

"I'm sorry." He frowned. "I didn't mean to frighten you."

"I—I was just—caught up in my thoughts. I'm okay, here." She offered him a small smile, hoping to put his mind at ease—and make him go away.

Far away.

"You're not okay according to the bride."

There was tension in his tone. Diana heard it.

"I have orders to get you out on the dance floor," he said. "Jane said you're a guest at her wedding, and she didn't want you to go home feeling as if you hadn't had a good time."

"B-but…I wouldn't think that at all," she rushed to assure him. "I am having a good time."

The idea of being held in Travis's arms, swaying to slow music had her desperate to get out of dancing with him. "I'll smile more," she continued. "I promise. I'll go over and introduce myself to…to…" Searching the room, she pointed to the first people she spied. "To that other couple over there."

"Won't do." Travis held out his hand to her. "Come and dance. Make the bride happy."

She knew her eyes expressed the panic she felt.

Softly he admitted, "Diana, I don't want to do this any more than you do. But—" he shrugged "—I don't see any way around it."

Looking from his handsome face to his out-stretched hand to his face again, Diana thought to protest further. But in the end, she figured he was right. She certainly didn't want to upset Jane on her wedding day. Diana knew her grandmother would tell her to do whatever it took to be gracious, grateful and hospitable. To give utmost respect to both the occasion and those being honored. It was the way of the Kolheek.

Sliding her fingers over his, Diana rose from the chair and allowed herself to be guided to the dance floor, all the while feeling as if she were being led straight to the gallows.

Think of other things, she told herself. Think of walking in the woods. Think of staring at the stars. Think of how, once this dance is over, you can march right up to the bar and order a stiff drink to steady your nerves.

Diana nearly groaned when Travis swung her around to face him. One strong hand settled on the small of her back, sending sparklike heat shooting up her spine, while the other one gently but firmly grasped her fingers.

He moved easily for a tall, broad-shouldered man. With sure steps never leaving a doubt as to who was leading, he steered her around the outskirts of the dance floor.

Diana focused on the other dancers, on the wedding guests who had chosen to sit this one out, on the children as they played near the front door of the banquet hall. She forced herself to direct her attention on anyone and anything other than the man who was holding her close.

Close enough to feel the heat of his body. Close enough to smell his cologne.

The heady scent of him brought to mind sensual images of romantic evenings. Of passionate kisses shared in the heat of the night.

Squeezing her eyes shut, Diana fought to swim her way out of her carnal musings. They were only going to get her into trouble. The thoughts swelled like a rising tide, threatening to drown her there and then.

Suddenly she sensed his attention on her, and helplessly she raised her gaze to his.

The need expressed in his dark eyes was brazenly unmitigated. Enough to steal away her breath. She felt captured. Mesmerized. And although their bodies didn't stop swaying to the beat, moving around the dance floor, she felt as if they stood stock-still. As though they were the only two people in the room. In the whole, entire world.

Diana clearly saw that he must have been suffering from his own arousing notions. The sweet misery of them was expressed in the tension of his jaw, in the slight flare of his nostrils.

It was as if their lips were connected by some

invisible elastic band that drew them, ever so slowly, closer and closer. She could feel his warm breath on her face, and the desire he felt was etched into every plane and angle of his ruggedly handsome face.

The moment seemed to hang in some kind of suspension of time. Hovering. Throbbing. Enticing.

Her heart fluttered like the wings of a frightened hummingbird, and her knees felt weak. Their lips were going to meet. Right here in this public place. In front of all these people. In the midst of all his friends. And there wasn't a single, solitary thing she could do about it.

The music ended. And the ceiling lights brightened a bit.

Still, Diana and Travis stood as if they were riveted to the floor. Riveted to the moment.

The lead singer announced that the band would be taking a short break.

Only at the sound of the man's voice did they breathe, and blink. It was almost as if they both awakened simultaneously from some strange, erotic trance.

"Damn," Travis whispered as he stepped away from her.

His Adam's apple bobbed in what looked to be a painful swallow. Diana thought that surely his throat must be as dry as her own.

She watched as his head swung around to survey the people closest to them. Evidently he was anxious about who saw what, and what those watching might have thought about the intimate encounter they had witnessed.

"Come on." His tone was gruff as he took her by the hand. "Let's go get something to drink."

At the bar, he asked her what she'd like, and she said, "A glass of white wine would be nice," not really surprised by the rusty quality of her own voice.

She didn't hear what he ordered for himself, but the highball glass he was served looked to contain something strong and straight. He took a gulp of the amber liquid. The huge breath he inhaled made his chest expand, and Diana's gaze watched his shirt-front tighten.

In an instant, an unbidden query arose in her mind as she wondered what his bare chest might look like, what it might feel like under her fingertips.

Stop! she commanded herself.

The wine barely seemed to have any taste at all when she took that first tentative sip. However, after the third taste, her knees felt less shaky and some of the giddiness had left her stomach.

"You know," he said after a moment, "I feel sorry for them."

Diana knew Travis was speaking about the bride and groom, about Jane and Greg, even without looking up from her glass.

"They're so damned happy right now," he continued. "But it won't be long before that'll change. And the change will take them by surprise. Before they realize what happened, they'll be bickering and fighting. They won't know how it happened, or why it happened. But it'll happen. It's inevitable."

"It's sad," she told him.

"It is." He nodded, then tossed back the rest of his drink.

She knew he thought she was agreeing with him. But in reality, she was expressing her opinion over the anger that was so obviously bottled up inside him. The hopelessness he harbored against love. Against relationships.

Diana knew she couldn't become involved in a loving relationship, that she had a problem that forbade her to allow a man to get too close to her. But that didn't mean she didn't believe in love. For others.

Helping Travis to believe, too, would be a wonderful gift she could give him. However, talking about man-woman relationships, discussing the beauty of love, without revealing her own unique problem might prove to be a little tricky.

If she were to put on her counselor's hat and remain uninvolved, she thought she might be able to succeed.

Remaining uninvolved would be the hardest part. She found the man physically attractive. Overwhelmingly so. But she could remain detached. She was trained. She could do this.

She shoved away the shadow of doubt that crept in to cloud her enthusiasm.

She could do this, her mind silently bolstered.

First, she had to discover the root of his problem. He had used his parents' divorce and his brother's broken marriage as reasons for not wanting to become involved himself. But Diana knew that people usually drew from their own experiences—their own *personal* experiences—when they made life decisions for themselves.

Sure his parents' divorce had impacted him. His

brother's unhappiness had, too. But rarely did individuals allow the problems and grief of others to influence them to the degree that Travis seemed to be affected.

There was more to Travis's determination than he was letting on. In order to make any kind of impression on him and his opinions, she needed to know the whole story behind what motivated his thinking.

She had to get him talking. About his past. Soon, he would reveal the entire truth behind his convictions against relationships. She decided that confronting the subject of divorce would be the best place to start.

"Sometimes," she began, not hindering the small smile playing across her lips, "I believe it might have been better to live a couple of hundred years ago."

He looked at her, curiosity sparking his gaze.

"Divorce was so much simpler back then."

Growing interest creased his brow, but he remained silent.

"For as far back as anyone can tell, the Kolheek was a matriarchal society." Her fingers slid up the stem of the wineglass. "The woman owned everything. There was no fighting over property. Or custody of the children. If a woman wanted a divorce, all she need do was set the man's only possessions— his moccasins, bow and quiver of arrows—outside the door of the teepee. He knew he was no longer welcome in her home."

"Wow," he breathed. "You're kidding."

She shook her head.

A chuckle rumbled from deep in his chest, and

helplessly, Diana found her gaze dipping to his shirt-front all on its own. Oh, how she would have loved to press the palm of her hand there, to feel the vibration of his laughter.

The sudden, out-of-the-blue urge made her breath catch in her throat and she gave a little choked cough. To cover the heat flooding her face, she lifted her glass and took a sip of wine.

"That custom sure would simplify things," he said. "And divorce rates would be through the roof."

"The casualness of Indian divorce did shock the Christian missionaries." The outside of the crystal glass felt cool against the heat of her fingertips. "But try to understand, early Kolheek marriages were not expected to be love matches. A young woman's mate was usually chosen by her family. It was a social contract made for economic reasons. A young woman might be married off to an older man to ensure her well-being."

From the intensity of his black gaze, he was completely engrossed.

"There is one tale of a young woman," she continued, "who was being pressured to marry a man who had done her father a great favor. Knowing that her daughter didn't want the union, the girl's mother consoled her by telling her that when she was older and knew better, she could marry whomever she pleased."

Travis was silent a moment, then he said, "See there. Even my own ancestors didn't believe in life-long relationships."

"Oh, yes, they did," she rushed to say. Then she actually winced as she remembered the story she'd just related. "Early marriages were a sort of...test. You know, for...experience. And sometimes merely for survival."

After a moment, she said, "You see, in great Kolheek tradition, young girls are taught that for every woman there is a man. One man. A great warrior who will love her. Protect her. Care for her. Provide for her. Each girl is determined to find her great warrior. Her soul mate."

This time, his laughter had a bitter edge. "That sounds a lot like the stories of white knights and damsels in distress. I guess every society has their fairy tales. Their cruel jokes and tall tales that set their children up for failure."

Driven by the overwhelming need to disagree, she said, "Oh, but the idea of having a soul mate isn't a cruel joke. And it isn't a fairy tale, either."

Diana was surprised by the vehemence with which she had spoken. She hadn't really realized the depth of her conviction about this belief until that very moment.

His dark eyebrows shot high. "So, you're looking for your great warrior, are you?"

Quietly she admitted, "I thought I had found him."

The words had slipped from her lips without thought. It was ironic that her goal had been to make him talk about his past, yet here she was on the verge of divulging more about herself than she ever meant to.

"You were married?"

Diana didn't see any harm in answering his question. It was the *reason* behind her divorce that she didn't want him—or anyone else for that matter—to discover.

"Yes," she said.

Softly, he guessed, "But you're not now?"

"No. I'm not now."

He waved to the barkeep for another drink. When the young man came to refill his glass, Travis pointed to her wine. "More?"

"No, thanks," she said. "I'm fine."

Leaning his weight on one elbow against the bar, Travis said, "I have to admit, I'm surprised. Most people who have been married and divorced exhibit a little more...angry negativity. Toward marriage, I mean. Divorced people are usually more angry. Blaming. Both my parents sure are. And my brother. What I'm wondering is why you're not."

Diana hesitated before speaking. He was exploring her past. Well, she'd take one more step toward making him understand, then she'd refuse to go any further.

"It's hard to blame my ex," she told him, "when I know that I'm the reason the marriage failed."

Okay, she silently told herself, she'd revealed far more than she'd expected to; however, she couldn't help but believe that it was necessary if she wanted him to confide in her the events surrounding his own experiences.

Her statement made him more curious than ever, she could tell, but before he could ask her any more about her past, she said, "You admitted your surprise over my optimism. Now, I have to admit something. When I brought up the subject of Kolheek divorce customs, I was hoping to get you to tell me why you're so...well, why you're so adamantly against relationships.''

It was clear that the directional change in the conversation made him uncomfortable.

''I told you,'' he said, at last, ''my parents went through a terrible divorce. My mother was angry. She's *still* angry. My father was shattered. And then my brother's marriage broke up. He was devastated by his wife's greed. It sure doesn't take a rocket scientist to figure out that...love stinks.''

Again, the depth of his bitterness shocked her.

''Maybe.'' She sipped her wine. There was more. She knew it. Was certain, right down to the marrow of her bones. ''But—'' her voice grew hushed as she speared him with her gaze ''—what I want to know is, how and when were *you* hurt by love?''

Clearly she'd stunned him with her question.

He murmured, ''Did your training as a Medicine Woman include Mind Reading 101?''

Diana knew he wasn't looking for a response. He was simply biding time. Gathering the shards of his wits that her question had evidently shattered like delicate glass.

He studied her. Hard. And she identified several different emotions as they crossed his expression. The first was resistance. Opposition. Like a stubborn mule, he clearly considered digging in his heels. He didn't want to reveal what he'd gone through.

Well, seeing that she was hiding a secret herself, she could certainly understand. But if she were to help him let go of his anger, she needed to know what was going on in his head.

Then she saw a spark of irritation. This, she knew,

was a simple defense mechanism, and as she expected, it quickly passed.

Finally his dark eyes softened with surrender.

"Okay," he said, "so I've lost at love. I wasn't the first, and I sure won't be the last. But I pity the fools who still play the game. All they're doing is setting themselves up for heartache. And I want no part of it."

"Travis, can't you hear how sad that sounds?"

"Maybe so. But that's the way it is."

She felt as if she were fighting a losing battle, and as is the habit of any underdog, she began grasping at straws.

"If you experienced the downside of love," she rushed to say, "then you must have encountered the upside."

"Not very much of it." He lifted his glass to his lips, swallowed. "And I've come to the conclusion that whatever upside I encountered was…all in my own imagination."

Diana expressed silent bewilderment, desperately hoping he'd elaborate.

He sighed. "I fell in love. I thought Tara loved me, too. But when I asked her to marry me, she laughed. Harshly. Right in my face. And then she proceeded to, ah, um…"

His words caught, then trailed as he swallowed. This was clearly difficult for him. After gulping in a breath, he continued, "She proceeded to divulge the names of several other medical students she'd been dating—sleeping with, actually—while she was seeing me."

"Oh, Travis. I'm sorry." She uttered the words in a horrified whisper. "That was cruel."

How awful for him. No wonder he harbored such anger in his soul.

"Well, you must have someone in your life who is a role model for healthy relationships." She looked up toward the front of the room where the bride and groom sat at the head table, laughing with guests. "There's Jane and Greg."

"And I've already told you exactly where I think they're headed."

His tenacity was frustrating.

"What about the relationship Greg had with his daughter's mother. Surely they must have had some good times—"

"Joy was the product of a one-night stand. Pricilla was, and still is, an angry woman who wanted nothing but to abandon her child. Greg agreed to raise Joy."

Diana's shoulders sagged. Then she decided to grasp at one more straw.

"What about Sloan?" she asked. "You said he's a widower. He and his wife…did they share a happy union?"

Something—humor or disgust, Diana couldn't tell which—tugged at one corner of Travis's mouth.

"Only if guilt, condemnation and self-reproach are healthy ingredients to what you call a happy union."

Unwittingly she found herself glancing over to where Sloan stood talking to his three daughters.

"Guilt and…?" She let the rest of her whispery question trail as confusion and curiosity churned in her brain.

When she gazed into Travis's face, he was shaking his head.

"It would take me a month of Sundays to explain," he said. "It was a complicated marriage. So complicated that the man is still dealing with the aftereffects."

She stared down into her glass, not even seeing the wine inside. Her thoughts whirled like a tornado.

This man didn't have one single person in his life who could boast a successful relationship. His parents, his brother, his friends. Everyone around him had experienced pain, anger, greed, guilt. How was she ever to counter all of that?

"So," he said, setting his empty highball glass onto the bar top, "no offence meant...but now you know exactly why I think all this talk about soul mates, great warriors and white knights is nothing but a bunch of hogwash."

Chapter Six

Snow flurries made Christmas morning perfect. Travis lit a fire and then started toward the kitchen.

"Shoo! Go away!" Diana waved him from the doorway with wide sweeping motions of her arms.

He chuckled. "I only wanted to help."

"But it won't be a surprise if you help," she said. "I'm doing just fine. Everything is nearly ready. Call the boys." Her face lit with a sudden idea. "Can I serve breakfast in front of the fire?"

"That's a great idea," he told her. "I'll spread a tablecloth over the carpet." He sniffed the air. Scents of cinnamon and molasses made him salivate. "Mmm, I'm hungry."

"Go!"

The mock sternness in her tone and in her nut-brown eyes made him laugh out loud. "I'm going," he said, inching away from the doorway. "I'm going-ing."

She sure did look good this morning. The black leggings encasing her lower body fit snugly, her turquoise silk shirt flowing to the top of her shapely thighs. Her hair was plaited in one fat braid, the very end adorned with an array of brightly colored beads.

He'd been thunderstruck by the intense moment they had spent staring into each other's eyes last night on the dance floor at the wedding reception. Holding her in his arms had simply been more than he had been able to bear. If the music hadn't ended, if the lead singer hadn't announced the band's break, Travis was certain he'd have caved in to his desire to kiss the woman.

The fact that he was so damned weak against the urge to touch Diana, to kiss her, had worried him. But after their talk, the one in which they had discussed her past and his, after they had talked about great warriors, white knights and soul mates—and he'd proclaimed the whole subject nothing short of bunk—he'd felt a little more in control. Voicing his opinion out loud had given him a sense of strength over his physical urges.

His flesh might be weak, but his conviction was still as solid as ever, he thought as he went to the linen closet to retrieve a tablecloth. He spread it on the floor near the hearth.

He hadn't been surprised to find that Diana had been married. She was an extraordinary woman, beautiful and intelligent. It was completely natural that some man had taken notice of that. Of *her*. What had surprised him, however, had been hearing that she blamed herself for her divorce.

What had happened?

The Silhouette Reader Service™ — Here's how it works:

Accepting your 2 free books and gift places you under no obligation to buy anything. You may keep the books and gift and return the shipping statement marked "cancel." If you do not cancel, about a month later we'll send you 6 additional novels and bill you just $2.90 each in the U.S., or $3.25 each in Canada, plus 25¢ shipping & handling per book and applicable taxes if any.* That's the complete price and — compared to cover prices of $3.50 each in the U.S. and $3.99 each in Canada — it's quite a bargain! You may cancel at any time, but if you choose to continue, every month we'll send you 6 more books, which you may either purchase at the discount price or return to us and cancel your subscription.

*Terms and prices subject to change without notice. Sales tax applicable in N.Y. Canadian residents will be charged applicable provincial taxes and GST.

If offer card is missing write to: Silhouette Reader Service, 3010 Walden Ave., P.O. Box 1867, Buffalo NY 14240-1867

NO POSTAGE
NECESSARY
IF MAILED
IN THE
UNITED STATES

BUSINESS REPLY MAIL
FIRST-CLASS MAIL   PERMIT NO. 717   BUFFALO, NY

POSTAGE WILL BE PAID BY ADDRESSEE

SILHOUETTE READER SERVICE
3010 WALDEN AVE
PO BOX 1867
BUFFALO NY 14240-9952

Play The *Lucky Hearts* Game

and get...
FREE BOOKS & a FREE GIFT...
YOURS to KEEP!

Scratch Here!
then look below to see
what your cards get you...

yes! I have scratched off the silver card. Please send me my **2 FREE BOOKS** and **FREE MYSTERY GIFT**. I understand that I am under no obligation to purchase any books as explained on the back of this card.

315 SDL C6KD   **215 SDL C6J7**

NAME   (PLEASE PRINT CLEARLY)

ADDRESS

APT.#   CITY

STATE/PROV.   ZIP/POSTAL CODE

Twenty-one gets you
2 FREE BOOKS and a
FREE MYSTERY GIFT!

Twenty gets you
2 FREE BOOKS!

Nineteen gets you
1 FREE BOOK!

TRY AGAIN!

Offer limited to one per household and not valid to current
Silhouette Romance® subscribers. All orders subject to approval.

Visit us online at
www.eHarlequin.com

The tiny question had gnawed at his mind all night like mice nibbling on the Christmas gingerbread.

The things that had happened during her marriage weren't any of his business. And with all these prideful thoughts of his renewed conviction, he shouldn't be concerning himself with her past. Nevertheless, the question continued to plague him.

"Let's eat."

Despite the quandary rolling around in the back of his mind, the singsong quality in Diana's voice had his heart feeling light. He nudged the boys away from the tree where they'd been busy checking out the packages.

"You're sure some of those presents are for us?" Jared asked, eagerness in his tone, excited anticipation twinkling in his eyes.

"I'm positive."

"And we get to open 'em after we eat?" the child persisted.

"You sure do."

Diana had wisely suggested that Travis spend some quality time with the boys before opening the gifts. That way their childhood memories would hopefully be focused on the day, on the togetherness, rather than the new toys. Travis had thought it a perfect tradition to begin the years of Christmas celebrations for his new family.

"Um...well...I'd like to know something."

When the usually quiet Josh spoke hesitantly, Travis took the time to kneel down on his haunches in order to be at the boy's eye-level. "What is it, son?" he encouraged.

"How did Santa know we were here?"

The awe expressed on the little tyke's face wrenched at Travis's heart. He smiled softly.

"Like I told you last night," Travis didn't hesitate to say, "Old Nicholas knows everything."

When he'd tucked the twins into bed late the previous evening, they had voiced some real concern over how Santa would know where to leave their presents. Travis had patted their little sleepy heads and assured them that everything would work out. Even after seeing the gifts under the tree when they awoke, the boys were still a little skeptical, it seemed.

The three of them sat on the cloth in front of the fire, and Diana passed out napkins while instructing them to tuck them onto their laps.

"If you don't mind," she said to them, "I'd like to say a prayer of thanks."

But she didn't actually say the prayer, she sang it. Her voice was rich and melodic, and it poured over Travis as if it were a pure and gentle rain. The words she spoke, he surmised, were Algonquian, the Kolheek's native tongue. He couldn't tell the meaning, but just hearing the tune caused an innate peace to settle over him. A seemingly perfect peace that he hadn't anticipated. Soon, though, she sang in English.

A shiver coursed through Travis. Not just from the prayer she was crooning, but from her dance as well. She circled them with graceful, hopping steps, her hands held heavenward, her chin tipped high. There was not a single nuance of self-consciousness in her movements. She was a beautiful sight to behold. In that moment, he felt proud of his rich heritage. And he felt grateful that Diana was here to instill that same kind of pride in his boys.

She expressed gratitude for the beautiful day and its momentous meaning, for the bounty of food set before them, for Josh and Jared's presence in Travis's home and then finally for Travis himself for taking on the raising of the twins.

Abruptly the air went still. Travis looked up to see Diana standing motionless, her eyes closed, as if she were waiting, seeking to hear something in what had become an almost sacred silence. The boys remained motionless and respectful through it all. Finally she opened her eyes and smiled.

"You guys ready to eat an old-fashioned Kolheek meal?" she asked the twins. They gave her an enthusiastic answer. First, she ladled out a steaming serving of cornmeal pudding and handed it to Travis.

"You have to remember," she told them, "white sugar wasn't available before the Europeans introduced it to us. Foods were flavored and sweetened with honey or sugar and syrup made from the sap of maple trees."

"I'd like a pancake, please."

"Actually, Jared," Diana told him, "these were called Journey Cakes. They cook up very quickly, and because they're flat, the cakes were easy to carry on long hunting trips." She focused on Josh. "And what would you like to try?"

"What's that wrinkled stuff?"

"Dried fruit. Want some?" When he nodded, she handed him the bowl filled with slices of apple, peach and pear. Then she offered him another bowl containing nuts and toasted seeds. She took some fruit and nuts for herself as well.

"During the spring and summer," she said, "when cherries and apples, peaches and berries are abundant, the women would set the fruit in the heat of the sun to dry. It was a way to preserve the fruit. That way, in the winter when snow covered the ground and not much food grew, the tribe had something to sustain them."

The pudding was warm and thick, something akin to Cream of Wheat or farina. The molasses flavoring was delicious.

They ate in silence for a time. Then Travis's heart lurched in his chest when he noticed the sparkle in Diana's eyes.

"And who wants some of this?" she asked the boys.

"Oh, boy," Jared exclaimed. "Popcorn for breakfast."

"Corn was terribly important to your ancestors," she explained. "Often, it kept the people alive through the long, cold winter. They boiled it, roasted it, simmered it in stew—"

"Popped it?" Josh asked shyly as he reached for a handful.

Diana nodded. "They also pounded it into meal to make pudding and mush and bread and fritters."

"Fritters?" Jared asked.

"It's a fried bread. Flavored with onions or spices, or sweetened and flavored with bits of fruit. It's delicious." She reached for a fluffy white kernel of popcorn.

"Sounds like corn was more than just important," Travis commented.

Diana nodded. Quietly she said, "It was sacred."

Jared had swallowed his last bit of Journey Cake, wiped his mouth on his napkin and looked longingly toward the glittering tree and all the brightly wrapped packages beneath it. Josh, too, cut his eager eyes to the far corner of the room.

Travis suppressed a grin at the children's obvious excitement and focused his attention on what Diana was saying.

"There are special dances," she continued, "and ceremonies, too, to celebrate corn. In college, I was fascinated to learn all the different Indian folk tales that explain where corn originally came from. I knew what the early Kolheeks believed, that a maiden descended from the clouds..."

Jared began to fidget. "So, um, when is breakfast over?"

Diana laughed, and the sound of it made Travis smile.

"Are you finished?" she asked Jared.

"Yup," he said, holding up his clean plate.

She looked over and saw that Josh, too, had finished. "Then breakfast is over."

The boys cheered as they scrambled to their feet and raced to the tree.

Travis caught Diana's eye. "I'm sorry the boys lost interest."

"It's okay." She leaned over to pick up the soiled dishes and her braid slid over her shoulder. "I can get carried away sometimes. It was silly of me to keep them when I knew they were anxious to open their gifts.''

On impulse, he reached out and captured the end of her long, plaited hair. The beads were smooth and cool against his palm. He tucked the braid back behind her shoulder where it would be safe from the sticky remnants of maple syrup and Indian pudding.

''I'm very interested in everything you have to say.''

She smiled, and his temperature seemed to heat up a few degrees.

''I know you are,'' she said.

The moment grew very still.

Suddenly she leaned her weight back on her heels. ''You know...''

Her words faded and Travis sensed a tentativeness in her. Then her chin tipped up a fraction.

''Maybe you'd like to have some instruction, too.'' One corner of her mouth inched back in a cute half grin. ''I know all this elementary information about food is probably boring for you, but—''

''No,'' he disagreed emphatically. ''I'm not the least bit bored. And I would like to know more. If you're willing to teach me.''

''Of course.'' Her eyes shied away from his and she busied herself with placing the leftover food on the tray. ''We can meet for an hour or so after the boys go to bed. Or, once they start school, we can talk before they get home.''

Softly he said, ''We'll work it out.''

''Yes,'' she told him, ''we'll work it out.''

The tautness of the air seemed to break with a silent sigh, and Travis got the distinct, almost uneasy, feeling that the two of them had just altered the course of things in some way. It was as if they had just surrendered to…something. Unknown. Intangible. Elusive. Whatever it was, he couldn't quite get a grasp on it. All he did know was that Diana was volunteering to instruct him in his Kolheek heritage. And he had a desperate hunger for the knowledge she'd offered to impart.

He reached out and took the dishes from her hands. "Let's go help the boys unwrap gifts," he said as he placed the plates and bowls on the tray.

"Oh." Her brow furrowed with consternation. "But I hadn't meant to intrude on your whole day. This is a day for family. I only wanted to show the boys some of the foods—"

"Will you stop," he gently admonished. "You're part of this family holiday." Then he smiled. "Besides, there may be a present or two under that tree with your name on it."

"Really?"

Utter surprise coated the single word. Then a childlike glee lit her gaze, and Travis chuckled. It was clear she hadn't expected to receive anything this morning. That made the time and effort he'd taken to choose a few gifts for her all the more meaningful.

A sudden thought crossed his mind.

"Do you normally celebrate Christmas?" he asked. He certainly didn't want to insult her beliefs.

Her smile was soft. "Christmas is a wonderful celebration that Kolheek children have come to love just as fervently as children all over the world. You see, The People are masters at weaving the old and the new into the blanket that is the Kolheek. We change. Adapt. Our people examine, and sometimes accept, new beliefs. It's what makes us strong. It's what has allowed us to survive.''

Thinking of his ancestors, of their history and ideology as a good, strong blanket was a wonderful concept. The notion that the blanket that was The People was still being woven, still being created, somehow gave him the first real inkling that he hadn't missed out completely. That he could still become a part of what it meant to be Native American.

The monumental revelation was enough to have his breath snagging sharply in his throat.

''Thank you.''

He was as surprised by his whispered expression of gratitude as she was.

''For what?'' she asked, her bewilderment evident.

But before he could answer, the boys called out to them. Their excitement could wait no longer.

An hour and a half later, Travis was sitting alone in the living room, bits of colored paper and curling ribbon here and there on the floor. He'd never experienced a Christmas quite like this one. Sure, he'd spent Christmases with Sloan and his girls. But he'd always arrived later in the day, when the gift-unwrapping frenzy was long over.

The boys had made this day so special. Their smiles. Their laughter. Their whoops of unrestrained joy.

''Cup of coffee?''

''Thanks,'' he said, accepting the steaming mug that Diana offered him.

She sat down on the far side of the couch.

"Although, rather than sitting here basking in all this relaxation," he told her, "I really should be straightening this place up. Sloan's going to be bringing the girls by in a bit."

With Greg and Jane on their honeymoon with little Joy, Travis and Sloan had opted for a short visit over a light lunch today rather than the full-fledged dinner celebration they usually shared together.

"There's plenty of time." She sipped at her own mug. "No harm at all in enjoying a second cup of coffee."

He breathed in the heady aroma, swallowed a mouthful of the creamy richness. "You know," he said at last, "I can't remember a time when I enjoyed a Christmas morning with as much enthusiasm as Josh and Jared enjoyed this one."

"That's the good thing about experiencing things through the eyes of children," she told him. "Not only do you get to enjoy the here and now of their fun, but their joy churns up good memories."

He laced his fingers around the heated mug. "Maybe I phrased that wrong."

Perplexity shadowed her gaze.

"What I should have said," he explained, "is that I never experienced that kind of joy at Christmas."

Her arched eyebrows crinkled. "Never?"

He shook his head, thinking back over time. Thinking hard. Then he shrugged. "Maybe I did very early on. But the Christmases I remember were fraught with disagreement and nit-picking that invariably turned into all-out arguments between my parents. Shouting and ranting that had me and my brother heading for our room. Unsettling memories, actually.''

"I'm sorry," she said.

He didn't know why he was telling her this. Her calm spirit just seemed to invite him to confide his innermost thoughts.

"It's a shame that your parents gave you those memories. Grown men and women should know better.'' Finally she said, "They must have been terribly unhappy with each other to act that way in front of their children. Maybe—'' her head tilted a fraction "—they never really belonged together.''

He sighed. Something she'd said made him want to pause. To take stock. To examine the past more closely in relation to what felt like the momentous statement she'd just made. However, more confession began tumbling from his lips, keeping him from pondering the moment.

"Once they divorced, things didn't get much better. My mother constantly and bitterly complained about how little my father contributed toward our gifts and our general expenses. And my dad would always call and complain to me about my mom keeping us from visiting him. I felt guilty for loving my dad. I felt guilty for loving mom.'' He heaved a sigh. "I didn't like holidays much.''

"That's understandable.'' A wayward strand of her sleek black hair had come loose from her braid and she absently reached up to tuck it behind her ear.

He suddenly felt uncomfortable, as if he'd put a damper on the day. "How about you?'' he asked, trying to brighten his tone. "What were your childhood holidays like?''

"Well," she began, "my grandparents made holidays special. You see, I never knew my parents. I've been told that my father had a problem with alcohol. He and my mother went out one evening. On the way home, my father drove their car into a ravine. Neither of them survived. My grandparents raised me." She smiled. "Spoiled me rotten, really. Especially on my birthday and Christmas. They didn't have much, but they gave me everything I needed."

Her smile was beautifully content.

"And lots of things I didn't," she continued. "I'm very blessed. Very loved." Seeming to steel herself with a deep inhalation, she said, "My grandfather passed away while I was at college. I miss him." After a brief pause, she murmured, "I loved him so much. He was the father I never knew. I think I married Eric with some subconscious hope that he could replace my grandfather." She shook her head. "What an awful mistake that was." After heaving a sigh, she said, "And then there's my grandmother…"

Deep affection and devotion were clearly expressed in the twinkle of her dark chocolate gaze.

"Well, you met her," Diana said. "She's quite a character."

Travis barely had time to chuckle in agreement before Jared came barreling down the stairs. Josh followed close on his heels, playing the wooden flute Diana had given him as a gift. She'd wrapped one for each of the boys.

"Would you show me how this game works again?" Jared asked, handing Diana the other present she'd given them.

Like the normal children that they were, they had tossed aside what they had initially perceived as hoe-hum strings of hole-ridden beads in favor of the more flashy electronic gadgets they had opened. But now both boys were evidently curious. Josh put aside the flute and crowded close to watch.

As she demonstrated how they were to swing the beads and attempt to catch them on the blunt-tipped needle, balancing as many beads as they could, one on top of another, Travis paid close attention to the three of them. Diana patiently explained that this was a game of skill that was hundreds of years old and how it was meant to develop a young warrior's eye-hand coordination and balance.

Incredibly she somehow got the boys to challenge themselves rather than each other. Competition was a good thing, Travis thought, but the twins were too young to be comparing their rudimentary skills to anyone else's just yet.

Josh and Jared giggled gleefully with each failed effort. Then Josh caught the second bead on his needle, balancing the first one on top of it.

"Wow!" Jared congratulated his brother. "How'd you do that?"

Josh beamed with pride. "Just lucky, I guess."

"It takes practice," Diana told them. "Lots of practice."

Reclining into a couch cushion, Travis sipped his coffee. And he marveled at the warmth that filled his chest. Not from the hot coffee he was enjoying, but from the joy and gratitude that filled him to the brim as he looked at his boys.

His life would never be the same.

And not just because of Josh and Jared. His life had been changed by Diana, as well.

She'd diligently guided the boys. She'd shown them things they might never have seen, taught them things they might never have known, had she not taken the time to come into his home and instruct them. But she'd influenced *him*, too. She'd reshaped some of his thoughts and opinions.

And for that he was thankful. And just as soon as he could, he planned to show her just how thankful he was.

The boys were tucked into bed, their first Christmas in their new home having been a day filled with new family, friends and loads of fun. A bright red fire engine sat on the floor by Jared's bed. He'd have had it under the covers with him had Travis allowed it. Josh was clasping the bead and needle game that Diana had given him. He'd had great fun in showing Sloan's daughters how he could catch the beads. Of course, he'd failed more times than he'd succeeded, but he hadn't lost interest in the challenge.

Travis gently took the beads from Josh's hand and lovingly tucked the blanket around his shoulders. He planted a gentle kiss on the forehead of one of his sons, then the other. After pausing for one last look at what he'd decided were his two greatest blessings, he closed the door and went back downstairs.

Toys were scattered here and there in the living room. He went to the tree with the intention of straightening up the mess. But first, he surrendered to the urge to have a little fun himself.

He held the needle of Josh's bead game and

flipped the beads with a small jerk of his wrist. Stabbing at the holes in the beads while they were in midair, he grinned when his needle came up empty. Again he swung the beads, and jabbed. And again he caught nothing. He chuckled.

"It really does take practice," Diana said. She came closer. "This was originally called the Needle and Bone Game."

"Bone?"

She nodded. "Deer toe bones were hollowed out and then holes were drilled in them before they were strung. The needle was made of either bone or wood." She grinned. "I almost told Sloan's girls about the toe bones when they were playing the game this afternoon. But I decided it wouldn't be nice to make them squeal in disgust."

Travis laughed softly. "Oh, but the boys would have loved to hear them shriek."

Setting the beads down on the coffee table, he looked up at the white lights winking on the tree. "This has been the most fantastic day of my life."

He'd had the thought several times throughout the day. Again, the tranquillity Diana presented made him feel at ease about repeating it.

"Those two little boys are a wonderful addition to your life," she said. "Each and every Christmas, from here on, will be just as fantastic."

Reaching up, he rubbed the back of his neck. He hated to doubt her. But there was something off about what she said. He'd have the boys for each and every Christmas, that much was true. But for some reason, he couldn't help but feel that no holiday would turn out as good, as deep-down-soul-satisfying, as this one had.

Chapter Seven

"I want to thank you," he said. "For...everything."

Travis's onyx eyes held an intensity that nearly made Diana weak. That awkward time of the evening had arrived, she realized. The time when their lesson was over, and they both seemed to get caught by the net of strain that invariably ensnared them.

For four nights in a row, they had met together after the boys had gone to bed. She'd begun his instruction by explaining tribal organization.

The basic Kolheek family unit, she'd explained, usually consisted of a father, a mother and their children. Although it was not uncommon for men of wealth to have more than one wife. Both father and mother treated their children with great love and attention. Corporal punishment was rare. Rather, when a child misbehaved the parents would reason over the problem and guide their offspring toward better conduct. The entire village took great interest in the raising of children, chastising misconduct whenever it was witnessed.

With ties of either blood or adoption, clans were members of elite families. Clan members of the Kolheek were descended through the female line. All members of a clan were considered brothers and sisters, so intermarriage was forbidden. Mates were chosen outside the clan. Each clan was ruled by a subchief. An insult to one member was considered an insult to all, and members of a clan would take to the warpath together.

A tribe included several villages made up of three classes of people. Nobles were members of clans and people of royal blood. Sannops were common people who made up the bulk of the community. And outsiders, or the lowly ones, who were little more than slaves, acting as servants to the two other classes. The Chief Sachem, always a member of the noble class, governed the tribe.

Travis, like most males, had been fascinated by her stories of combat. And she'd spent the past two evenings explaining war traditions. Just as the needle and bead game she'd given the twins was meant to develop certain skills, other games Indians played were intended to emphasize a warrior's best battle qualities: daring, self-reliance, agility, strength, endurance and bravery. The center field of any village became a proving ground for a brave's future war glories.

Although all young men were allowed to witness the war dance, they could not actually participate until they were sixteen. And even then they had to

prove their maturity and self-reliance by surviving a
test. Led blindfolded into the wilderness in the dead
of winter, the young man had to survive armed only
with a bow and arrows, a hatchet and knife. The
following spring he would return to the village and
his appearance would determine his success or failure.

Tonight she had explained how any minor prov-
ocation between tribes could trigger a war. Insults
were instant fuel to spark the fire of battle. Cruelty
and lust for bloodshed had nothing to do with it,
she'd stressed. Honor was key in any war.

The night before a battle there would be a war
dance. Large bonfires would flicker against the night
sky as excitement rippled through the crowd of gathered warriors. A hush would fall as the war chief
stood to address the group. If the war party was large
enough, the Chief Sachem himself might lead the
event. Small parties were headed by an inferior chief-
tain. But no matter who addressed the men, the
speech would be heartfelt as the leader asked for vol-
unteers and spiritual guidance to ensure success.

Following strict tradition, the attacking tribe would
forewarn the enemy with arrows planted near the target village, and the attack was usually made at dawn.
Prisoners were occasionally adopted in place of a
slain warrior. Once accepted, he would take the place
of the deceased, whether son or husband. If a pris-
oner wasn't adopted into the tribe, he faced death by
slow and terrible torture.

She'd finished up the lesson on warring by de-
scribing the spears, arrow points, knives and clubs
used for battle. She'd showed him some of the books

she'd brought with her from the reservation, and he'd marveled over the drawings of New England Indian weaponry.

Diana stared at Travis, feeling, as always, very awkward at his effusive gratitude at the end of each lesson.

"I wish you wouldn't keep doing that," she said.

"Doing what?"

"Thanking me…" Then she added, "Like that."

He frowned, his ebony eyes shadowing. "Like what?"

"You know." Nerves had her chuckling and averting her gaze. "So…I don't know…copiously. It makes me uncomfortable. I enjoy talking about our heritage. You don't need to…" Self-consciousness got the best of her and she let the rest of her sentence die away.

They had gotten along so well since she'd offered to instruct him, to educate him about his heritage. They had laughed together. And she loved that he was so interested in his ancestry. He'd asked interesting questions and made intelligent observations. The time they spent together was a joy. She really wished they didn't have to suffer through these few stiff-as-a-board moments each night before they parted.

"Making you uneasy wasn't my intent," he said. Out of the blue, he slid his palm over her hand. "I just need you to understand how very important all this is to me."

Heat spiraled in her stomach. His skin was warm against hers. Protective. And that feeling made her feel panicky.

No, she realized, it wasn't really his touch that made her feel so suddenly anxious. It was the words accompanying his touch. The intimation that his gratitude and his touch suggested.

Her thoughts were suddenly one big jumble, pieces of a puzzling idea flying hither and yon in her mind. Something momentous was happening in her head. Something she needed to work out, but she sure didn't want to do it here in front of Travis.

"I'm tired." She blurted the announcement as she stood up. "I'm going to bed. Good night."

Without giving him a chance to reply, she rushed from the room, up the stairs and into her bedroom. And it wasn't until the door was firmly closed behind her that she felt safe enough to examine the chaos that had welled up inside her so unexpectedly when Travis had reached for her.

They had acknowledged the attraction they felt for each other. But they had also professed determination to ignore the lure they experienced.

Why, then, did Travis continue to look at her with such focus? With such intent? His dark eyes seemed to hold some mysterious meaning. Some strong purpose.

And why did he have to thank her each night? His gratitude seemed sincere, but it sparked all manner of chaotic emotions in her.

Somehow, someway, the fact that Travis continued to look at her with longing and his effusive appreciation were connected. She could feel it. However, hard as she tried, she wasn't able to splice together the link that would make it possible for her to solve this unsettling quandary.

* * *

Early the next morning, Travis found Diana in the kitchen fixing herself a cup of tea.

"Morning," he said. A thrill ran though him at the sight of her. Still, after days and days he'd spent with her, he was amazed at how he was affected by her. Even with her hair sleep-tousled, her face devoid of makeup, she looked lovely to him. Just lovely.

He was nervous. He hadn't slept much. The problem that had oh-so-slowly presented itself since Christmas day still had him confused, and he'd decided in the wee hours of the morning that he wouldn't find peace until he discussed these amazing thoughts running around in his head with the person responsible for planting them.

Diana.

Just looking at her made his gut grow all tight and knotted. He continued to have this tremendous physical reaction to her even after all the mental lectures he'd given himself, even after they had openly come to the decision that neither of them was interested in a relationship. And now he finally thought he'd figured out why.

This relentless corporal response—and the connection it had to something she'd said on Christmas day—was what he felt the tremendous need to discuss.

"You're up early."

"Yes," he said. "I wanted to get the coffee ready for us. Maybe I'll whip up a little breakfast."

She set the used tea bag onto the saucer beside her cup. "Sorry, but I don't really feel like breakfast at the moment. I didn't even feel like coffee this morning. Tea will do me just fine.''

He noticed for the first time that she looked pale, her face strained. "Are you feeling ill?"

"No. Just tired." Without explaining further, she picked up her teacup. "If you don't mind, I think I'll take this up to my room. The boys won't be up for a while yet—"

"They won't," he agreed in a rush. "And I was hoping you'd be up. So we could talk."

Some emotion flashed across her face, and for a moment he thought she was going to refuse him.

"Please, Diana," he said before she could withdraw from the conversation completely. "I have something I want to tell you."

The sigh she expelled was small, resigned, and she took her cup and saucer to the table, pulled out a chair and sat down.

His nerve endings danced and jumped as he was walloped with anxiety. She was sitting there waiting to hear what he had to say. How could he make her understand all that had been churning through his mind for days now when he hadn't even been able to work it all out for himself yet? Well, he'd worked it out. At least, he thought he had. Although he still couldn't quite believe the conclusions he'd finally reached.

He'd decided just hours ago that he needed to confront Diana with his thoughts. Tell her about his change of opinion. His change of heart. However, he was worried about how she was going to respond.

"Just give me a second to get the coffee brewing."

The few moments it took to measure out the ground beans and water then flip on the switch of the electric coffeemaker gave him just enough time to calm his thoughts a little.

With one deep and bracing breath, he went to the table and slid down into the chair nearest her. He didn't dare touch her, although he wanted to. However, he didn't want to frighten her with the magnitude of all he was thinking and feeling. Instead he folded his hands on the table in front of him.

"The first thing I want to say," he began slowly so as to keep his wits about him, "is that I've never in my life met a more extraordinary woman. You're helping my boys. You're helping me. And no matter what the future might bring, I want you to know I'm grateful."

Was that suspicion narrowing her gorgeous cinnamon eyes? he wondered. How could she possibly have trouble believing him? He was speaking with the utmost candor. With his heart wide-open.

After a moment of silence, she seemed weary as she said, "You thanked me last night, Travis. And the night before that. And the night before that. I told you last night that this isn't necessary." She slid her chair out an inch. "If that's all you wanted to talk about—"

When she started to stand, he reached out and gently touched her sleeve.

"No," he said, "that's not all."

Although she remained seated, she tensed. He could feel it in the muscles of her forearm, in the very air around them. Reluctantly she lifted her gaze to his.

"You said something on Christmas day that started me thinking," he told her. "What you said...well, it's changed everything for me." He didn't understand the stress she so obviously felt, but he quickly decided that his own nervousness was probably triggering her tension.

"We were talking about my childhood holidays," he continued. "About how my parents fought and argued."

"I remember." Her tone was whisper-soft.

"What you said was that my parents didn't belong together."

Mild alarm had her mouth forming a small circle. "Oh, but I certainly wasn't passing judgment on them, Travis. You must believe me. I was simply making an observation."

"I'm not upset by what you said," he told her. "How could I be when all you did was speak the truth?"

It was clear to him that she had no clue where he was going with this conversation. He had so much he wanted to say. But he didn't dare attack her with his awesome conclusion just yet. He had to work up to it. So she'd understand.

"You said at the wedding reception that..." He stopped long enough to take a breath. "You said that the Kolheek teach their little girls that there is a great warrior, a man who is meant only for them."

There it was again, he thought. That suspicion that clouded her gaze.

"And you promptly told me that was hogwash."

He chuckled softly. "I do remember my response."

The smell of coffee filled the kitchen, but Travis barely noticed it so intent was he on releasing all the thoughts that were churning inside him.

"Tell me," he urged her, anticipation surging through him. "Tell me what *your* grandmother told *you*. Did she speak of your soul mate?"

Diana nodded. "Of course she did. All women talk to their daughters about love. It's like telling your children about the birds and the bees. About sex. The story isn't complete without the chapter on what a physical relationship means."

"What did she say?" he asked, excitement building in him. "How did she say you would recognize the one man who was meant only for you? How you would recognize your soul mate?"

"How I would recognize…" She shook her head, her voice dragging into silence. "Travis, I don't understand what this is all about."

"Just tell me." His fingers curled around her wrist as he strove to keep his eagerness at bay for just a bit longer.

Diana looked toward the ceiling, evidently trying to remember. "She didn't really," she said, lowering her chin to look into his eyes. "All she said was that I should listen to my heart. That I'd know." Her tone lowered as she repeated, "That I'd just know."

"And did you feel that way with your ex?" he asked. "That he would be your mate for life?"

Her cheeks flamed. "W-well, I don't know," she stammered, averting her gaze.

Disconcerting her hadn't been his motive. The self-consciousness she so obviously felt made him uncomfortable, but he simply had to know her thoughts at the time of her marriage.

"I—I didn't really think about it. I was a child when my grandmother talked to me of such things." She shrugged. "I met Eric. I was still grieving my grandfather. I'm afraid I didn't take the time to listen to my heart. Eric and I seemed to get along. Getting married just seemed the thing to do." Her cheeks tinged an even deeper pink and her tone seemed to compress even further as she said, "I wasn't one to sleep around."

"So you married him..." he spoke slowly, voicing his thoughts as he spoke them "...not because you were looking to replace your grandfather, but because you wanted to experiment with sex—"

"Of course not!"

She tried to pull away, but he held her fast.

"Please don't be embarrassed. I'm only trying to work this out."

"Work what out?" Anger sparked in her eyes now. "I don't understand why you're saying these things."

"What I'm trying to figure out," he said, the tumult he'd been holding back suddenly rushing forth like floodwater through a broken levee, "are the feelings I keep experiencing. Amazing feelings. Incredible feelings. For you, Diana. And I'm trying to figure out how my feelings for you fit...how they relate to what you said about my parents. About them not belonging together."

All she did was shake her head and stare at him wide-eyed.

No wonder. He wasn't making a bit of sense.

He took a deep breath. "Listen, I believe with all my heart that you were right about my parents. I believe they never belonged together. That's why they separated and divorced. It was inevitable. I believe that my brother and his wife never belonged together, either. Tara and I didn't work out, because *we didn't belong together.*"

Sheer excitement had him inching toward her. He cupped her elbow with his free hand.

"You separated from your husband because the two of you weren't soul mates." He moistened his lips. Softly he said, "You didn't belong together."

Her eyes were large, conveying an odd mixture of confusion and disbelief, but Travis didn't let that stop him from making his point. He eased himself closer to her, and the lemony scent of her skin smelled more erotic than anything he'd ever experienced in his whole entire life.

"And because of the way I feel about you," he whispered, "because of the strong physical reactions I keep experiencing, I think that—"

He leaned even closer.

"—maybe—"

And closer.

"—we...do."

"Do?"

He didn't know if she'd actually spoken the tiny word or simply mouthed it, but he felt her sweet, warm exhalation brush his cheek and a shudder quaked through his whole being.

"Belong together," he breathed against her mouth.

And when he pressed his lips to hers…he felt as if he'd finally come home.

Her mind seemed to have completely short-circuited. Travis had moved closer and closer, all the while voicing this almost farcical notion about soul mates and belonging together.

Nothing made sense. Nothing at all.

The delicious pressure, the luscious taste of his mouth against hers…the heat of hands on her back and in her hair…only made her brain, her thoughts, all the more snarled and confused.

Mere days ago, he'd been so sure he didn't want to act on the attraction that plagued them. He'd had good, solid reasons motivating his desire to remain unattached, free of strings and relationships. He'd flat-out declared that he thought her idea of a great warrior, of everyone having a soul mate, was total nonsense. He'd said it.

He'd believed it.

So why the sudden turnaround?

You're an extraordinary woman, he'd said. *You've helped my boys. You've helped me.*

After those statements, he'd once again declared his gratitude. With a huge amount of resolve and intent.

You're an extraordinary woman. His words echoed in her head yet again. *You've helped my boys. You've helped me.*

The puzzle pieces swam in the mire that was her thoughts. A few of them snapped together. The budding image was fuzzy, but her gut told her that the picture about to be revealed wasn't going to be pretty.

Her hands trembled and she clenched her fingers, afraid to move her hands for fear of reaching out to hug him to her. His tongue skittered across her lips. The warm scent of him nestled around her like a blanket. She was sure that while he was so close, kissing her, touching her, she'd never untangle her thoughts.

Planting her palm flat against his chest, she pressed. It didn't take much effort to push him away from her.

The desperation she read in his eyes was the final piece of the puzzle that clicked into place. She'd been right. The picture wasn't only *not* pretty...it was downright ugly.

"Don't do this to me, Travis." Her voice was as rusty as weathered nails, and her throat actually hurt as the words grated from her. "I've been a novelty. And novelties wear off. I won't put myself through anything like that again."

He did a great job of looking surprised.

"Novelty?"

His dark head shook back and forth with the perfect amount of bewilderment. A more naïve woman might have been taken in by his act.

"What are you talking about?" he said.

She stood up. So did he.

"Look," she told him, "I'm happy to give the boys—and you, for that matter—all the instruction I can while I'm here. I'll tell you all I know about our heritage. All I ask is that you refrain from playing games with my feelings. I don't know what kind of wild notion you've got in your head, but I won't allow myself—''

"Whoa," he said. "Stop. It's pretty clear that you don't understand."

"I understand perfectly," she told him. "Just a few short days ago, you told me that you didn't believe in loving relationships. That you were sure that your friend and his new wife…that Greg and Jane were going to end up divorced and hurt." She pointed an accusing finger at him. "You told me that you didn't believe in love."

Her breath came in big gasps.

"Yet, once I begin to meet with you, once I try to make you understand what it means to be Kolheek, you come up with this idea that we need to be together." She poked herself in the chest with her index finger. "I'm not stupid. I can put two and two together and come up with four. You want me around because you think I'll be good for Jared and Josh. That I'll be a good influence on them. Give them the grounding they need. The grounding that *you* need." Her narrowed eyes would have wounded him had they been daggers. "You want me because I'm Kolheek!"

"Diana, listen to me—"

But when he stepped toward her, she backed away. And the look on his face couldn't have registered more surprise if she'd have swung out and slapped him. He went utterly still.

"Eric thought it would be really neat to have me around. I was just a little different from the other women he'd met. A novelty. But the newness wore off. Fast."

She felt her anger flash in her eyes like lightning. And she did all she could to keep the electricity alive. Anger was good right now. If she allowed it to fade, she'd cry. And she'd rather die than reveal her true feelings—her pain, her tears—to Travis right now.

Why she was hurting so much, she couldn't say. All she did know was that she felt as if her heart was being ripped right out of her chest.

"I want to do all I can for Josh and Jared while I'm here. And for you, too," she said. "But, I'm begging you...don't use me."

Chapter Eight

"So, um, we was wonderin'..."

Jared's tone was tiny and uncertain, as though he wasn't quite sure if he should speak his thoughts aloud.

Travis had been extremely upset by what had transpired between himself and Diana just moments ago. She'd completely misconstrued the motive behind his idea that he and she just might be meant for each other.

He realized his change of thought—his change of *heart*—regarding relationships and love was staggering. It had taken him days to come to terms with it, so it was no wonder she hadn't believed him. But the notion she'd drawn from his suggestion...that he only wanted her because of her background, because of her heritage, was ludicrous.

He'd been desperate to explain. To make her understand. And when she'd bolted from the kitchen, he'd followed her, calling out to her all the way to the stairs.

But he'd been stopped in his tracks when he saw the twins descending in their pajamas, worry marring their small brows, shadowing their gazes.

"We been awake," Jared had announced, tossing a quick glance at his brother who had stood on the bottom step beside him. "And me and Josh have been talkin'."

Travis hadn't seen any other recourse than to let Diana escape. The sound of her bedroom door closing had forced his eyes shut for the briefest moment. He'd talk to her. He'd straighten things out, but his boys needed him. That much had been obvious.

He'd brought them to the couch, waited for them to climb onto the cushions and then he knelt down in front of them so they would be face-to-face.

"Now," he said quietly, placing a hand on one of each of the boys' knees, "what's this all about?"

"I had a bad dream," Josh admitted.

Travis was surprised that he was the one to speak up first. Usually it was Jared who talked for the both of them.

"Is that what you want to talk about?" Travis asked. "Your bad dream?" He could tell the child was frightened, so he used a gentle voice hoping to coax Josh to talk.

Josh only shrugged. Then he said, "Sorta. I guess."

Jared nudged his brother. "Tell 'im, Josh. Go on."

Josh's big, dark eyes grew even more troubled. "I thought I woke up back home. You know, back with the other kids. Back...there."

"At the orphanage?" Travis supplied.

Josh only nodded. "I couldn't find you. And then I couldn't find Diana. Then…"

The watery tears that welled in the boy's eyes ripped at Travis's heart.

"Then I couldn't find Jared." With a quick swipe of the back of his hand, Josh dashed away the teardrop that rolled down his cheek. "But then I woke up. It was a dream. A bad dream. I didn't like bein' alone, so I woke up Jared."

"I don't want you to ever feel alone, Josh," Travis told the child. "The next time you have a bad dream, you come to me. Even if it's the middle of the night. You wake me up. Helping you through the scary times is an important part of my job as your dad."

"Once I was awake," Jared said, taking up the story, "we started to talk. And…well, we need to know somethin'. We need you to tell us."

Travis nodded. "I'll tell you anything you want to know."

The boys looked at each other and Travis got the distinct impression they were passing some sort of silent message meant to bolster their courage. Finally the twins focused on him.

It was Jared who spoke. "How come you brung us here?" he asked. "How come you want us?"

Travis thought to correct the child's grammar, but then thought better of it. Jared needed the freedom to say what was on his mind, never mind what words he used, just so long as he made himself understood.

After a brief moment, Josh solemnly added, "Yeah. How come you wanted us when nobody else did?"

Travis didn't move. He didn't dare. The insecurity on their young faces, wrinkling their tender brows, was enough to make his throat swell with emotion that was hot and thick. But seeing him break down wasn't what these boys needed at this moment. They needed him to be strong. And sure. His answer would have to be meticulous. Wise and reasonable. Understandable. Good enough to make them feel safe for all time.

These children where so innocent. Not yet six. Yet they had suffered physical pain and mental anguish enough to last them a whole lifetime. Travis wanted to prevent them from experiencing even another instant of heartache.

It was a foolish notion, he knew. Jared and Josh had a lifetime ahead of them...a lifetime that would be fraught with trials and errors as well as joys and successes. He couldn't keep them from sorrow and failure. He could only love them. And be here to help them up whenever life knocked them down.

Where on earth, he wondered, would he find the words that would take away their uncertainty where he was concerned? How could he make them understand that he would be here, permanently and without fail, for as long as they needed him?

"Why did I want you?" His voice was raspy, like bits of metal that had been shredded and twisted out of shape. He stopped long enough to swallow around the lump in his throat.

"There's this thing," he slowly began again, "called fate. You can't see it. And you can't touch it. So it's a really hard concept to understand." He looked from one set of dark eyes to the other.

"But—" he paused, searching for words "—I want you to try. See…fate makes things happen. Fate brought us together. You were all alone. And I was all alone. And fate thought we'd be good together. Fate thought we'd make a good family."

Jared's face brightened with the explanation, but deep-thinking Josh had more questions in his eyes.

He asked, "Do *you* think we make a good family?"

"Absolutely," Travis was quick to answer. He pushed himself up and then slid in between the boys. "What do you think, Jared? Do you feel we make a good family?"

With his head bobbing furiously, Jared said, "I sure do. I like it here. I like our new house. I like our yard. I like our swing set out back. I like our room. I like my new bed. I like…I like *everything.*"

Hardly able to breathe, Travis asked, "How about your new dad? How do you feel about me?"

Jared darted a shy glance at Travis. "I don't really *like* you." He shrugged. "I kinda love you."

Unable to quell the warmth surging through him, Travis hugged the boy to him. "I kinda love you, too, Jared."

But Travis knew it wasn't Jared who had the biggest problem with anxiety. Jared was easygoing and had little trouble adapting. Swiveling his head to meet Josh's gaze, Travis asked, "How about you, son? How do you feel about being here?"

Josh blinked, once, twice, before he spoke. Finally he said, "This is the best place I've ever been."

Now, taking into account that the boys hadn't been anyplace other than the orphanage and the hospital,

Travis knew the statement—to someone who didn't know better—wasn't worth a whole bunch. However, the overwhelming emotion that came rushing behind the words made the proclamation very weighty indeed.

The knot in Travis's throat swelled and he thought it would be impossible for him to speak. But there was more to say. So much more.

"That's good, Josh," he said, intricate emotions snarling the words. "Because there's no place else I would rather you be than right here with me. See…I love you, son. I love Jared, too. And I want you and me and your brother to be a family. You think we can do that?"

"I want to. But…"

"But what?"

"How come I keep having bad dreams?"

"That's pretty normal, I think," Travis told him. "You're getting used to a new home. Once you really understand that this is where you belong, I think the nightmares will stop bothering you."

"I tried to tell you," Jared said, leaning over to peer at his brother. "Santa can't be wrong."

"Santa?" Travis couldn't keep the surprise out of his voice.

"Yeah," Jared continued. "Santa wouldn't have left our fire engines here if he didn't think we were supposed to be here. I told Josh that this morning."

Suppressing an indulgent smile at the delightfully simplistic answer and the wonderful display of youthful faith, Travis looked down at Josh and nodded in agreement. "Your bother's got a point. Santa can't be wrong."

Travis only wished all of life's problems could be answered as easily.

Sitting out of sight at the top of the steps, Diana listened as Travis attempted to allay the boys' fears. She'd been so upset by her confrontation with Travis that she'd raced up the stairs past the boys without even having acknowledged seeing them. However, once she'd reached her room and she'd had a moment to calm herself, she'd worried that her behavior might have upset them. So she'd crept from her room, back down the hallway to make sure Josh and Jared were okay.

Travis had done a wonderful job of making them feel safe and secure. He'd made all the correct moves; he'd listened to them with deep concern, he'd spoken with quiet sureness in his most convincing argument that here was where he wanted the boys to be.

Travis was so patient with the twins. So kind. He had all the perfect qualities that went into making a good father. Most important, he loved those children. And he'd do anything for them. Anything. That was so very clear to her.

Over the past few weeks that she'd been here, he'd proved time and again that he'd do whatever it took to make their lives happy, give them whatever it was he thought they needed for their well-being.

And she'd just realized that one of those things was *her*.

The idea that he was seducing her in order to provide the boys with their Native American heritage and traditions sent cold chills raking down her spine like fork tines.

Would he really treat you so poorly? The question filled her with sudden doubt as it whispered across her brain.

But then her chin trembled with chaotic emotion. *Yes,* she silently decided.

He would. He was a man, wasn't he? And men always showed their true colors. Sometimes it took months, as it had with Eric. Sometimes it only took weeks, as it had with Travis.

But months or weeks, in the end, their true personalities would show through.

She hated to think badly of Travis. Hated to think that he'd lie and manipulate her in order to give the boys the grounding they were so sorely lacking. He knew they needed a firm foundation that was rooted in the past, a foundation he wasn't able to provide. She hated to think he'd take advantage of her like this.

But there was something else she hated. Something she despised above all else. And that was realizing at this very moment—knowing in the very core of her heart—that she'd fallen desperately and deeply in love with the man when he only wanted to use her.

Travis fixed breakfast for the boys, and while they ate, he'd showered and dressed for work. His patient schedule was light for the day so he'd be home in time for lunch. However, he didn't want to leave his talk with Diana until the afternoon. He simply couldn't.

Once he'd come downstairs to find the boys watching a favorite cartoon video, he'd asked them if Diana had come downstairs. Both of them said they hadn't seen her.

There were two reasons he trudged up the steps toward her room. One was that he didn't want her thinking such appalling things about him for one moment longer than was absolutely necessary. The other was that, if he didn't clear up her misconception of his motives before he left this morning, he'd be so preoccupied with the awful things she thought about him that he wouldn't be able to focus on his patients' needs, and that wouldn't be professionally responsible behavior. He needed to straighten out his personal life so he could give himself completely to the patients who depended on him.

Lifting his hand, he knocked softly. There was no answer.

"Diana," he called. "We need to talk."

He waited. All he heard was silence.

Finally he said, "You know that I have patients this morning. And I know you've made plans with the boys. But I'm not leaving this house until you hear what I have to say."

Ten long seconds passed before he heard the knob turn, and then the door opened. The doubts and fears shadowing her dark eyes tugged at his heart, made him want to reach out to her. But he didn't.

Instead he walked past her and seated himself in the big, overstuffed easy chair. He looked over and saw that she hadn't moved from the doorway, her hand still poised on the knob.

"Come over here," he said, the soft request in his tone unmistakable.

She hesitated, looking over her shoulder out toward the hallway. "But the boys…" she said, letting the rest of her thought linger in the stillness.

"They'll be fine," he told her. "They're watching television." He patted the bed's coverlet. "Come. Sit. I've got something to say…something you need to hear."

He'd purposefully emphasized the word need. Yes, she needed to hear his thoughts. But he also had a terrific need to speak them.

She moved to the bed and perched herself on the very edge of the mattress. Immediately he got the impression that if he were to say one wrong word, she would jump up and flee. Her nervousness was apparent, and he knew he'd have to tread softly or she'd never stay long enough to hear him out.

The tension in the air snapped, but he ignored it, refused to get caught up in it. Instead he leaned over to rest his elbows on his knees and he gazed steadily at Diana. She seemed so close, merely inches from him. But judging from the apathetic expression she struggled to exhibit, he felt as though she was determined to lock her emotions so deeply inside her that she might as well be miles away. He was determined to reach her. He was overcome with the sense that his happiness depended on it.

"I don't really know what I've done," he began, "to make you think such terrible things about me. But I want to assure you that you're wrong. Completely wrong about my motives."

The clouds in her eyes were unreadable.

"I don't know what happened between you and your ex," he continued. "But from what you said this morning, I have the feeling that the man thought it would be fun, or unique, or cool, or unusual, or whatever adjective works here, to be married to someone of a different ethnicity than himself."

She remained statue-still.

"If that's so…" He let the words hang in the air while he sighed heavily. "If that's so, then that's very sad for him. Because that means he wasn't able to look past your genetic profile to see the real you. The person inside. The wise and wonderful woman that you are."

A flicker of reaction. An almost imperceptible narrowing of her eyes. It was enough to set his heart hammering against his ribs.

"But what's saddest about the situation," he said, "is that you were hurt by that worthless son of a—" The magnitude of his sudden swell of anger made him stop short and he pressed his lips together tightly, letting the rest of his thought go unspoken. He paused and consciously released the fury in a small puff of breath. Only then, did he continue. "I think you were made to feel as if you weren't worth having. And that just isn't so."

She actually blinked then. However, doubt still shadowed her gaze.

"Now, I don't know how you came to the conclusion that I only wanted you because you're Kolheek, but that argument is like a sieve that won't hold water because—" here he let his voice grow soft "—honey…I'm Kolheek, too."

"But you haven't experienced what it means to be

Indian,'' she told him in a rush, evidently thinking that this somehow substantiated her thoughts. "I can give the boys—''

His frown was deep as he stopped her with an upraised hand. "You think this has something to do with Josh and Jared?'' He straightened in the chair. "Honey, what I'm feeling for you—what we feel for each other—has absolutely nothing to do with the boys. And if you're honest with yourself, honest about the emotions we've been experiencing, you'll admit that I'm right.''

Stubbornness firmed her chin, her lips compressing with her obvious refusal to agree with him. Okay, he thought, so she wasn't going to admit it out loud. But he knew she was slowly and silently coming to acknowledge his claim. Her resolve was cracking. He could see it in her eyes.

"I won't sit here and try to make you think,'' he said, "that your being Kolheek has nothing to do with what I'm feeling. Because it may have a lot to do with it.''

She blanched, and for a moment it was clear that she meant to close herself off from him again. But before she could wall up every bit of herself from him, he reached out and touched her sleeve.

"You are the most beautiful woman I've ever met.'' The fabric of her blouse felt whispery-soft under his fingertips as he slid his hand up her forearm and then back down to her wrist. "Meeting you. Hearing the things you have to say about—'' He cut off the thought, but then forced himself to say "—about *our* people has opened up a whole new world for me. You make me feel as if I've...I don't know. As if I've found refuge. As if the possibility for vindication is…is…available.'' Immediately he corrected, ''Not only available, but *imminent*.''

The bewilderment wrinkling her brow gave him pause.

''Vindication?'' When she shook her head, a lock of her silky black hair fell across the back of his hand.

Travis moistened his suddenly dry lips. ''You see…''

He stopped. Took a deep breath. What he was about to reveal wasn't going to be easy. He'd never told anyone what he'd done all those years ago. But now he felt a tremendous need to confess. He needed Diana to know and understand. But he wanted so desperately to tell her everything without offending her in any way.

Start at the beginning, a small voice echoed from the back of his mind.

''When I was young, we never talked about my mother's Native American heritage. My heritage. And to this day, I can't tell you why. My mother refuses to talk about where she came from. Refuses to discuss her family.'' He lifted both his hands, palms up, in a gesture meant to convey his bafflement. ''Neither I nor my brother ever made a big deal about it. We simply grew up thinking of ourselves as proud Americans. Nothing more. Nothing less.''

Reaching up, he pinched his chin between his fingers and averted his gaze, unwilling to witness the disappointment in her eyes when she discovered his folly. ''However, when I was a senior in high school,

I was encouraged by a guidance counselor to use my
Native American race as an edge when applying to
colleges. An edge that would open more doors for
me where educational scholarships were concerned.
I desperately wanted to attend college. And medical
school. So I did it. I used my Native American heritage.'' He swallowed, then leveled his gaze on her.
''And I feel guilty as hell about it.''

Confusion continued to mar her forehead and
cloud her gaze. ''But—''

''I certainly meant no disrespect,'' he blurted.
''And as soon as I was able, I began doing some
reading about…about The People.''

Why did that phrase continue to stick in his throat?
Maybe because he didn't feel worthy to be a part of
his own rich heritage?

''I contacted the Kolheek reservation,'' he continued. ''I registered as a member. I…I've wanted to
be a part of…of…'' He shook his head. ''But I never
felt as if they'd…as if I…''

Frustration got the better of him.

''Travis.''

Her soft voice was like a magnet that drew his
gaze to her face.

''You're speaking as if,'' she said, ''well, as if you
aren't a part of The People.''

''That's exactly how I feel. As if I'm an outsider
looking in.''

''But your mother is full-blooded Kolheek,'' she
said. ''That makes you Kolheek, too. It doesn't matter that your mother—for whatever reason—doesn't
want to recognize her Indian heritage. Refusing to
honor and appreciate your birthright doesn't make it

null and void. Your mother is still Kolheek. You are still Kolheek."

Warmth spread all through his body, and Travis identified it as pure happiness.

"I've been slowly coming to that conclusion," he explained. "And you are the reason that I have. You've made me feel that I can be a part of what it means to be Indian. And that...and that I won't be turned away."

He noticed that the wary woman who had been sitting before him moments before was gone, and in her place sat the calm counselor, the nurturer, the Medicine Woman who was concerned for nothing but his welfare.

"You think because you haven't grown up on the reservation," she said, "that the Kolheek would reject your desire to know more about your ancestry? That we'd decline you access to us?" Her eyes turned gentle. "We couldn't do that. You are who you are. You're Kolheek."

"But—"

"No buts," she interrupted. "Travis, there are more Kolheek people living off the reservation than on. There are Kolheek living all over this great country of ours. Some living abroad, too. You can't feel guilty simply because you used who and what you are as an edge. You can't feel guilty about not knowing much about your history. You're doing what you can to make up for that."

He felt grateful for her wonderfully convincing argument.

"In fact," she continued more softly, "I think that maybe I have an idea. Something that might make you feel more a part of, more embraced by your ancestry. How would you like to take part in the naming ceremony?''

He didn't understand. ''But, as the boys' father, won't I be a part of it all?''

''Of course. But I'm talking about you having your own ceremony. You acquiring your own Kolheek name.''

A chill coursed across his skin and the small hairs at the back of his neck raised. ''But isn't the ceremony just for children?''

One of her shoulders lifted a fraction. ''Usually. But aren't you still in the infancy of discovering your past?''

He couldn't stop the smile that crept across his mouth, nor could he quell the emotion that misted his eyes. This woman was wonderful. She was astonishing. And he knew at that very instant, that Diana was the woman he wanted to spend the rest of his days with.

''I—I...'' He halted, hoping a deep and steady breath would help him to speak around the knots of emotion churning in his chest, rising in his throat. ''I'd be honored to have a Kolheek name.''

''Good.''

Her smile was like golden sunshine.

Now, he decided, it was time for him to finish what he'd come up here to say. It was time for him to make her understand.

''Because you came into my home,'' he said, ''because you were willing to give Josh and Jared the very thing I never had, a solid foundation in Kolheek tradition, because you were willing to instruct me, I *have* begun to realize that I can be a part of it all. I can be proud of my heritage. And that wouldn't have happened had you been anything else but Kolheek. That's what I meant when I said just a few moments ago that I can't say your being Kolheek doesn't matter.''

Panic paled her beautiful face. Clearly she hadn't expected the conversation to once again become so intimate so quickly.

"However," he forced himself to continue, "it isn't the Indian heritage that attracts me. It's the woman. It's the person you are. It's the caring, loving individual who sets my heart to racing each and every time we're together.''

He clenched his teeth, scared to death to reveal the full truth, yet determined to go through with it. Now that he'd finally figured out just what Diana meant to him, he wanted her to know exactly how he felt.

"It's the very essence of you—" his voice sounded rough and grating even to his own ears "—that I've come to love. That's what brought me to the conclusion that we're soul mates.''

There it was again, he saw. That defensive shield was being raised, like an impenetrable drawbridge meant to safeguard a castle from attack. The Medicine Woman was nowhere to be found. The counselor, the teacher, the mentor was gone. Dissolved like acid-splashed silk.

All he perceived was a frightened woman who seemed desperate to protect herself.

Chapter Nine

He loved her. Oh, heaven forbid. Is that what he'd said?

Yes. Yes, it was. And realizing that made her knees feel like warm rubber. Joy flared inside her chest like bursts of fireworks. Yet at the same time, she seemed overwhelmed with a frenzy of panic.

Deep down, she'd known that she'd been wrong about his motives. Even while she'd been conjuring her misconceptions about why he'd changed his mind, she'd been plagued with a whispery doubt. Her subconscious knew he was an honorable man. And he'd been nothing but right when he'd said he—someone of Native blood—couldn't be compared to Eric. There's no way Travis could have meant to use her ethnicity when he was of the same race as she. The idea was ludicrous to say the least.

So why had she misjudged him? Why had she

trumped up those charges against him? Why had she deliberately misconstrued his motives?

She knew why. Oh, she knew why. It was a last-ditch effort to save herself from utter humiliation.

"I'm sorry." Her apology was exhaled on a murmuring breath. "I'm sorry I hurt you. I'm sorry I accused you of trying to use me. I know it's not the truth. I know it."

Chaos whirled in her mind. She didn't want to reveal her own motives. She didn't want him—or anyone, for that matter—to know the truth about her.

"I'm actually glad you changed your mind about…" The phrase hovered on the tip of her tongue, and she was afraid she might not be able to bring herself to speak it, but she bolstered herself and said, "Loving relationships."

The intensity in his shining, crow-wing eyes forced her to look away.

"I had hoped that you would come to see that relationships…well, that they're a very important part of a person's life."

"I do see that now," he told her.

Still, she was unable to look at him. She felt quivery, off-kilter.

Why? Oh, why was this awful trick being played on her? Why did Travis have to enter her life, plead his love for her, when her only recourse was to deny him? It was like some cruel and inhumane joke.

"I'd believed from the very beginning," he said, "that fate had brought Jared and Josh into my life."

"I know you did."

"I don't understand how I could have been so

blind to the fact that fate brought *you* into my life, too.''

The silence was stentorian. The very air felt as though it pulsed and throbbed. She lifted her gaze to meet his.

''But fate brought Tara into your life, too. Just as Eric was brought into mine.''

He didn't hesitate to answer, ''She was a test. A lesson. And your ex was your test. Your lesson.''

Diana had known the point she'd attempted to make was thin at best.

''Those relationships were good examples,'' he continued, ''of what love isn't.'' He chuckled softly. ''I guess we're a little thick. It took us both a while to learn.''

She wished she could join in with his laughter. But the pressure of knowing what she would need to do was weighing heavy on her shoulders.

''Actually,'' he said, ''I probably wouldn't have learned at all, if you hadn't been here to teach me.''

Did he have to be such a remarkable man? Did he have to be so kind and generous? How was she ever going to turn him away?

The task would be easy, she suddenly decided. All she had to do was think of the humiliation she'd suffer if she didn't. All she had to do was imagine the disappointment she'd eventually see in his eyes if she did anything other than renounce his idea that they were meant to be together. That they were soul mates.

Soul mates.

The phrase rustled through her mind like a warm, gentle breeze through silky hair.

The mere idea that she'd found her great warrior would have to be enough for her. For living without him would be the only way for her to save face. She could live the rest of her life in peace, content in the thought that Providence had not completely shunned her.

"Diana."

As he spoke her name, he reached out and touched her knee with an intimacy that clipped her breath to the quick. If she didn't get away from him, away from his dangerous touch, surely she'd suffocate.

"No, Travis." She brushed his fingers from her, stood and walked to the window. "It cannot be. What you're looking for from me, I'm not able give."

She reached out and drew back the sheer curtains and gazed out at the back lawn where she'd enjoyed hours of play with the twins. She'd made wonderful memories here. Memories that would have to sustain her for the rest of her life.

"I don't know why you're saying this," he said.

Diana kept her eyes on the view of the yard and the trees beyond.

"But I suspect it has something to do with your failed marriage. I think you're suffering from some kind of residue left over from the hurt you received at the hands of your idiot ex-husband."

She sensed that he shifted his position in the chair.

"Whatever it is, Diana," he implored, "we can work it out."

Shaking her head, not taking her eyes off the horizon, she said, "No. This can't be worked out."

Before she even realized it, he was behind her. His

hands on her shoulders were like fire that blazed straight through the fabric of her blouse to blister her skin. However, rather than feeling the need to escape the heat of him, she longed to lean back, to be consumed in the flames they sparked.

"What I don't understand—" his mouth was close to her temple, the rich sound of his voice resonating in her ear "—is how you can blame yourself for the failure of your marriage."

The warm scent of him wafted all around her, enfolding, enveloping.

"This man you married." Derision was thick in his tone as he spoke the noun. "If his love for you wasn't pure, as you've indicated it wasn't, then the fault of the relationship's failure lays on his shoulders. Not yours. I don't understand how you can think otherwise."

She sighed. "It's not as simple as that, Travis. Such things rarely are."

"Then explain it to me."

Using gentle but firm pressure, he turned her to face him, and panic made her heart flutter, her stomach knot.

"Help me to understand."

The pleading in his eyes wrenched her heart.

"We deserve to be together," he said. "I can feel it in my bones. I think you feel it, too. I know you do. We both have. From the very beginning. Tell me what happened to you. Tell me why you won't…"

His frustration was obvious. And as she looked into his handsome face, into his kind eyes, she knew she had to tell him. He deserved the truth. He'd grown so over these past weeks. Rebuffing him with no explanation simply wasn't fair, or noble, or just. She knew she had to do right by him.

Standing where she was, between him and the window casing, she felt too hemmed in to talk comfortably about this most uncomfortable subject. So she slipped away from him and went to stand near the dresser a few feet away.

"I won't say that Eric's behavior didn't hurt me," she began. "But our marriage was falling apart long before the novelty he felt in having an Indian for a wife began to wear off." She stopped long enough to take a slow, nerve-steeling inhalation. "And the divorce really was my fault." A shadowy smile played across her lips. "Although I do appreciate your trying to make me believe something different."

She laced her fingers at waist level, then unlaced them. "You see, I...I have a problem. I don't enjoy..." Heated embarrassment flooded her face. "I don't respond t-to normal..."

Surprisingly, hot tears welled up in her eyes and her chin trembled with deep emotion. She didn't want to say this. She didn't.

But he wouldn't understand if she couldn't force the words from her throat.

Her gaze dropped unwittingly to his burgundy dress shoes and she barked out a harsh and humorless laugh. "As Eric so enjoyed telling me—I'm frigid. I can't respond to a man the way a woman should." She forced herself to raise her eyes to his. "I have...sexual inhibitions."

He looked shocked. Completely taken off guard.

As though she punched him right in the gut when he wasn't looking.

Finally he said, "Diana, I—"

"No." She cut him off by spinning in a half circle, embarrassment cocking her head, hunching her shoulders. "I don't want to talk about it, Travis. It's…it's utterly humiliating for me. You have to see that." Her breath was ragged, but she managed to continue. "I only wanted you to understand. You deserve that much."

Movement on the periphery of her vision had her darting a glance at the mirror she now faced, and she realized she could still view him from where she stood.

He stared off at a far corner of the room, his handsome face portraying nothing less than unadulterated astonishment. The emotion bit deep into his brow, paled his skin, tightened his jaw. The incredulity he felt seemed of such magnitude that it led him, silent, down the only path available to him.

Shaking his head, he walked out of the room. Only then did Diana allow her pent-up tears to flow.

Travis sat at his desk, staring with unseeing eyes at the files in front of him. He couldn't believe what Diana had told him. He couldn't fathom that she thought she was sexually inhibited. He'd kissed the woman. He'd touched her. He'd held her in his arms. Passion had fairly simmered in her. He'd felt it.

The knock on his door was enough to startle him from his deep and troubled thoughts.

"Hey, pal," Sloan called to him, pushing his way into the office.

Acknowledging his friend with a nod of greeting, Travis said, "Come on in. Is everything okay?"

"I came in here to ask *you* that." Sloan pointed over his shoulder toward the outer office area. "Rachel and the nurses...they're a little worried. Something wrong at home?"

Travis would have loved to confide in Sloan. Talking out his thoughts regarding Diana's problem might make the idea easier to deal with. But he couldn't help feeling her doubt about her sensuality was too intimate to share with his friend. It was clear that Diana hadn't really wanted to tell Travis. She'd be mortified if she were to discover he'd revealed to anyone the things she'd said.

"It's nothing I can't handle," he said, hoping he sounded more confident than he felt.

Sloan nodded. "Okay. But if you want to talk..."

"Thanks, buddy." Thinking it best to change the subject, Travis said, "I haven't seen the girls in a few days. How are they?"

"Good." Sloan's broad smile revealed a lot about his love for his daughters. "We're still arguing about the New Year's Eve party they've been invited to."

"You're going to let them go, aren't you?"

The man shrugged. "I guess so. But I refuse to let them stay out half the night. What parent invites kids to a party that lasts until three in the morning? It's ridiculous."

"It's only one night," Travis couldn't help pointing out.

One of Sloan's dark eyebrows shot high. "I'll remind you of that when your boys are on the verge of becoming teens."

Travis had to chuckle. Then thoughts of Diana—
and her astonishing revelation—seeped into his
thoughts, making his smile wane.

His astute friend knew him too well not to notice.
"You sure you're okay?" Sloan asked.

"Listen," Travis said. "What would you do if
someone...well, if someone thought something about
themselves that you knew wasn't true?"

"Is this a patient we're talking about? Or one of
the boys?"

Rubbing anxious fingers over his jaw, Travis said,
"Let's just say this is someone important."

Sloan only nodded, not pushing further. Travis
knew his friend would discern and respect his need
for privacy in the matter.

"I need more information," Sloan said. "What is
it this person believes about himself?" He quickly
added, "Or *her*self, as the case may be."

"I, ah, I really can't say." Without thinking,
Travis reached out and snagged a pen from his desk-
top, rolling it nervously between his fingers. "Let's
just say someone you knew to be quite intelligent
thought she wasn't. Or...or she thought she wasn't
pretty when you knew damned well she was not only
pretty, but...quite striking."

Sloan came closer to the desk and lowered himself
down into the empty wing chair. "Look, I've talked
to Diana. I know she's an educated woman. And
she's self-assured, and she's—"

"Who said we're talking about Diana?" The de-
fensiveness in his tone nearly made Travis cringe.

With his mouth drawn into a straight line, Sloan

only stared. But Travis refused to break Diana's confidence.

Reining in his misplaced irritation, Travis said, "If you don't want to help me out—"

"Of course I want to help you out." Sloan sighed. "Okay, if I found myself in the situation you just described, I'd do whatever I could to convince…this person…that—" he paused, evidently considering his words carefully "—well, that she is smart and beautiful. No matter what misconceptions she might have about herself."

A ray of light seemed to shine on Travis. What a perfect idea!

He murmured, "Convince her…"

Sloan nodded. "That she *is* what she thinks she isn't."

Travis was ready. After dinner, he'd scoured the books Diana had provided him, and he'd been able to come up with just the right questions to lead the conversation the way he wanted it to go.

Sure, manipulating the dialogue might not be considered a decent thing to do, but his motives were more than honorable. He planned to help Diana see that she was a beautiful, desirable woman who was filled to the brim with passion. Before this evening was over, she'd realize she was nowhere near inhibited where sex was concerned. She'd also be forced to realize that the two of them definitely were soul mates.

After he'd closed the bedroom door on his sleeping sons, Travis stopped in his room for the two books he'd been reading. He went downstairs in search of his Medicine Woman. He found her enjoying the lights on the Christmas tree.

"I guess we'll have to dismantle the tree soon," he said softly.

She tensed visibly the instant she realized he'd entered the room.

"The needles will soon be drying out and falling off."

She barely nodded in response.

"I've been reading the books you gave me." He moved toward her and he was taken aback when she actually sidled a half step away. Maybe this wasn't going to be as easy as he'd thought. "Could I ask you a few questions?"

"I'm not sure I'm up to it tonight, Travis."

He gently caught her arm as she passed. "Just give me a few minutes of your time. Please?"

There was a frantic instant where he was certain she meant to refuse him. Then the determination in her gaze seemed to hover as her indecision wavered. And when it waned, he sent a silent prayer of gratitude heavenward.

Shrugging her arm from his grasp, she said, "Okay, but just a little while. I—I'm really tired this evening."

He was terribly disappointed when she sat in the chair flanking the couch.

Moving around the coffee table, he said, "It would probably be best if you sat over here next to me. That way, we could both see the book."

Again, her face clouded with hesitation. Sitting beside him was the last thing she wanted, that much was clear. But, again, she yielded to his request, and he felt jubilant, as if he'd won the first of what might prove tonight to be many battles.

He spread open the book on his lap to the page he'd thought would make a good opening to his planned conversation.

"I was surprised," he said, "to learn that not all Indians lived in tepees."

The picture depicted a beautiful cone-shaped tepee, the tanned skin covering decorated with boldly colored symbols; rainbow stripes and a buffalo head.

"That's a stereotype we can thank Hollywood moviemakers for," she said. "Although, most of those old John Wayne movies did take place in the Old West."

Her smile warmed his heart. The moment she began to talk about her favorite subject, she began to relax.

"The plains Indians of the Midwest lived in traditional tepees," she continued. "They were portable, so the tribe could move to find food or to escape enemies. Indians of the southern plains, the Sioux and Cheyenne, used three foundation poles. Crow and Blackfeet Indians lived further north and used four poles. The hides of buffalo were tanned and smoked so that they'd be waterproof but still remain soft, and the hides were wrapped and laced with pins carved from willow wood. Willow is flexible."

When she leaned closer to the book, a long lock of her glossy black hair fell across his thigh. His gut tightened.

She pointed to the buffalo head. "Those are symbols of the Blackfeet," she told him. "They were meant to protect the family living in the tepee from sickness and bad luck.''

Her eyes lifted to his, and all trace of the awkwardness she'd been feeling was gone. Her dark gaze was clear and glistened with keen interest.

''You see, Native American dwellings came in all sizes and shapes.'' Absently she tucked the strand of hair behind her ear. ''Cones, domes, triangles, squares, rectangles. And their names were just as varied—chickees, hogans, igloos, tepees, longhouses, lean-tos, wickiups. Being part of the Algonquians, the Kolheek lived in wigwams. Shaped like an oval dome, it was constructed of saplings that were placed in holes made in the ground. The new wood was malleable enough to be bent at the top and tied together. More saplings were placed around the sides and top to reinforce the structure. The frame was covered with mats woven of cattail rushes.''

''That sounds fine for summer. But wouldn't that make for chilly living in the winter?''

''During the coldest part of the year, the outside walls would be covered with bark.'' Again, she leaned toward the book, turning a page or two. ''Birch was used whenever possible. Birchbark is lightweight and could be rolled up easily if the tribe had to move.''

The warm-lemon scent of her wafted around him. ''Fascinating.'' And if asked if he were commenting on the information she was providing or simply on *her*, he'd have no trouble telling the honest-to-goodness truth.

She looked up from the pages and smiled. ''I think so, too.'' After only a moment's pause, she said, ''I thought this book had a picture of a wigwam, but it doesn't look like it. I could go upstairs—''

Placing her fist on the cushion between her thigh and his, she made to rise, but he stopped her with a light touch.

"That's okay," he told her, the pressure of his fingers urging her to remain where she was. "I can see it later. I have other questions."

Focusing on the book, he turned to a particular page. A male and female were dressed up in wedding finery.

"We've talked about clans and families," he said. "And how marrying within the clan was forbidden. So…how did men and women meet? And once a man had his eye on the woman of his choice, how did he go about wooing her?"

Diana gave a tiny shrug. "All the tribes and bands would gather together fairly often for powwows, or seasonal celebrations. I'm sure the young men and women spent a great deal of time during those gatherings in search of a suitable mate. I would guess even older men and woman, widowers and widows, would have done the same thing. Having someone to spend your life with was important. Just as it is today."

Seeming to suddenly realize the topic, Diana's gaze took on a tentativeness, an uncertainty that brought out in her an unmistakable vulnerability. Travis's protective instinct stirred to life.

"Once a man and woman felt a mutual—" she paused long enough to swallow, her speech coming slower "—a mutual attraction, they would visit together outside the female's wigwam. They'd pull a blanket over their heads so they could talk with some semblance of privacy while still being chaperoned. I—I can imagine they didn't like being stared at by others.''

''I can easily understand that, too.''

Their gazes seemed riveted, locked tightly together. She moistened her lips, and he could tell she wanted desperately to look away. But, evidently, she couldn't.

Neither could he.

''Another courting ritual…''

Her voice was sweet and vibrant as warm honey, and it flowed over him, through him.

''…involved the playing of love tunes on a flute. In the dead of night, the young man would creep outside his love's wigwam and he'd serenade her.''

Suddenly her luscious, full lips contracted into a wry smile that struck Travis as the sexiest sight he'd seen in ages.

''Of course,'' she added, ''if he had no musical ability, he could always give her a gift. A basket he'd woven. Or a necklace of beautiful beads he'd strung.''

''Ah.'' Now it was his turn to offer an ironic smile. ''So jewelry has been coveted by women for thousands of years, huh?''

''I guess you could say that.''

He felt breathless, as though every molecule of oxygen had disappeared from the very air around them. If he didn't reach out to her, if he didn't touch her this very moment, he was sure he wouldn't survive to see the sun rise.

Her bronze cheek was softer than the finest silk,

and he oh-so-slowly ran his fingertips back toward her delicate ear. The pearl earring she wore was simple as adornments went, yet it symbolized her perfectly. Just like a pearl, she was a rare and precious find.

"I don't weave baskets," he told her softly. "And I don't string beads. So how in the world am I to let you know how I feel?"

She reminded him of a tiny bird, so obviously wanting to flee, yet too frightened to take flight. Her mouth was poised in a small, silent circle as he placed his lips against hers.

The kiss was sweet, and it was hotter, Travis thought, than the scorching flames flickering in the hearth. It would have been easy for him to lose all control, to shove aside the book resting on his lap and deepen the kiss. Heaven knew, he certainly wanted to do all of those things. But that would have defeated his purpose. That would have completely crushed his aim.

For his plan to succeed, he knew that Diana had to be the one who took the kiss to the next level. She must be the one to reach out to him. She must be the one who elevated this simple kiss to something more.

For a brief and heart-haunting moment, he thought she might not take the bait he was so blatantly holding under her very nose. But then he planted one more kiss—soft, delicious and terribly chaste—on her lips, and it suddenly seemed as if the dam of passion he knew was inside her burst at the seams.

Reaching up, she laced her fingers deep into his hair. Her nails raked his scalp as she pulled him toward her. Her lips parted, and her tongue darted out to dance sensuously with his.

His pulse drummed in an ancient, erotic beat. She tasted faintly of wintergreen, hot, delectable and tempting as hell itself. He could get lost in her, he knew. And that could happen easily. But losing himself was not his objective. Proving her passion *was*.

Curling his fingers around her slender wrists, he gently tugged her hands away from him, disentangling her fingers from his hair. He did his damnedest to ignore the deep-rooted disappointment that welled up in him as he extricated himself from her grasp. She broke off the kiss and leaned back to look at him.

The desire sparked in her chestnut eyes nearly defeated all his good intentions. He was dangerously close to chucking his plan altogether in order to enjoy what clearly could be glorious moments in her arms. But in the end, honor won out. He wanted to help her. He honestly did.

Her breath came in gulps, and she swallowed, immense confusion contorting her brow.

"Don't you see, Diana?" he asked her. "Don't you see that you're a passionate person? A sexual being?"

She blinked, evidently getting used to the idea that the erotic moment had passed. Silently she searched his face. Then...as his questions sunk into her mind, her eyes went wide with, first, surprise, then, red-hot anger.

"How dare you?" She scrubbed at her still-moist mouth with the back of her hand. "I can't believe you would do such a thing."

Her rage was so intense, her voice grated with it. Travis was completely taken off guard by the extent of it.

She stood, her hands clenched at her sides in small, bloodless fists. "I am *not* some science project for you to be experimenting on. I will not be treated—"

"Wait. Just hold on." He held up open palms. "I only meant to help…I wanted to change your mind…I wanted to make you see—"

"What you made me *see*…is that you are a heartless and cruel man. And I refuse to stay in your house a moment longer than I have to." With that, she bolted across the room.

"I—I wanted to s-show you," he stammered, shoving aside the books and standing up. But he let the rest of the thought trail when she didn't slow down.

He'd only meant to change her mind about herself. And reveal his deep feelings for her. At the same time.

But, somehow, his plan had backfired. Dreadfully.

"Diana!"

She stopped at the bottom step and turned her cold, angry gaze on him.

"What about the boys?" he asked. "What about the ceremony?"

"I don't intend to disappoint the boys. They'll have their naming ceremony just as I promised them they would." Fury fairly pulsed off her small frame. "I suggest you keep the gathering small. If you invite only your closest friends and family, the boys and I can be ready in three days."

"But that'll be New Year's Day," he pointed out.

"Seems appropriate to me," she said. "New names on the first day of a new year. And after the ceremony is complete, I'll be leaving your house, Travis Westcott. And if anyone cared to ask me, it will be none too soon."

Chapter Ten

"So, are you telling me that you think Jane's condition is operable?" Travis couldn't believe what he was hearing. Last month, Greg had inferred that his lovely wife had balked at the idea of marriage due to her inability to give Greg children of his own. She'd agreed to become his wife only after Greg had lovingly assured her that baby Joy was the only daughter he needed. But now Greg was saying Jane's infertility might not be so permanent after all.

Greg had returned to work this morning after his short honeymoon in the Bahamas with Jane and little Joy. He was tanned, and grinning like only a man who was happy and content with life could. Travis felt a sharp pang of jealousy. Never in a million years had he thought he'd want to be married. Now, spending his life with Diana was an idea that had been pestering him of late. To think that he'd actually jeered at the concept of matrimony at Greg and

Jane's wedding reception on Christmas Eve, and now he was feeling envious of what the couple shared just days later.

"I'm saying it *could* be," Greg told him from across the conference table. He sipped at his morning coffee. "We won't know for certain until she visits the gynecologist. But from what she described to me, her monthly cycle seems to be functioning perfectly. And from all she's told me, the doctor she saw at the clinic never really gave her a solid diagnosis. He just told her what he thought might be her problem."

"Why in the world would a doctor make a woman believe she was barren when he hadn't performed any tests to back up his theory?"

Greg only shrugged. "You have to remember, the clinic she visited was for low income patients. Working part-time as a waitress, Jane had no insurance. And no money to pay for even the most inexpensive tests. Could be that the doctor was doing his best with the situation he was handed."

"Or he could have been a complete quack."

"Could have been," Greg softly agreed.

Travis spent a moment trying to take it all in. Finally he said, "Wow, I'll bet Jane is ecstatic."

Although Travis thought it impossible, Greg's smile brightened even further. "She's over the moon. But she's trying to contain her excitement. So am I. We don't want to set ourselves up for disappointment. We're going to take it slow."

They sat in silence for a moment, sipping coffee and nibbling at the warm muffins Rachel had so graciously brought them this morning. They were waiting on Sloan to arrive for their morning consultation.

"So, what's been happening around here this week?" Greg asked.

"Well, Sloan's girls were in the office while you were gone," Travis told him. "They jumped all over their dad about the party."

"Is he going to let them go?"

Travis nodded. "He says so. If he doesn't, I think Rachel just might step in and talk to him. She's cares an awful lot about those girls."

Setting his coffee mug down on the conference table, Greg leveled a serious gaze on his friend. "You think Sloan has any idea how Rachel feels about…?"

Before Greg could finish his question, Travis was shaking his head. "The man hasn't a clue."

The men grew quite again. Finally Travis said, "Listen, if you, Jane and Joy haven't planned anything on New Year's Day, I'd like for you to come to the boys' naming ceremony."

Surprise made Greg's eyebrows shoot upward. "I thought that was to take place later in January. Closer to the twins' birthday."

Travis hesitated. "It was. But…Diana has decided to return home…sooner than she'd expected." The idea of her leaving Philadelphia, leaving his life forever, had him feeling desolate inside.

His head cocked at a slight angle, Greg asked, "Okay, what did you do?"

"It's all Sloan's fault."

"What's all my fault?" Sloan pushed open the door and set his briefcase near one of the empty chairs.

"You were the one—" Travis couldn't keep the

accusation out of his tone ''—who came up with that brilliant idea to convince her she...well, that she's a passionate woman.''

''*What?* But *you* said—'' Sloan pointed at Travis's chest ''—she thought she wasn't pretty. That she thought she wasn't smart.''

''Well, I couldn't very well tell you the truth, now could I?''

''Why not?'' Greg innocently asked. ''Seems you just did anyway.''

Travis's jaw jutted. ''Nevertheless, Sloan's advice was that I should convince her that she was what she thought she wasn't.''

''But—but,'' Sloan stuttered.

''Boy,'' Greg murmured, ''this whole place went to hell in a handbasket while I was gone.'' He grinned up at the two men. ''So, Travis, did you convince her?''

''I tried. And now she's not only offended, but she's also determined to leave.'' Travis knew his misery was apparent as he added, ''And I don't want her to go.''

Both his friends speared him with sharp, curious gazes.

Amazement glazed Greg's expression and his words as he commented, ''Sounds to me like our hard-hearted Travis has been bitten by the love bug.''

''And if he has been,'' Sloan added, ''he's in deep doo-doo. Because even rabies shots won't cure that ailment.''

''I don't want a cure.'' Travis rubbed his fingers over his chin. ''I just want to convince Diana to stay.

But I'm afraid there isn't time. After New Year's Day—''

"What's happening on New Year's Day?" Sloan asked.

"She's performing the naming ceremony," Travis explained. "I'd like you and the girls to come, if you can."

"We'll be there."

Greg quickly assured, "We'll all be there."

"Thanks." His appreciation was heartfelt. His friends had never failed him.

"Listen," Sloan said, "what do we bring the boys? Money? A gift?"

Travis shook his head. "You don't bring anything. It's custom for us to give you gifts. Out of respect. For agreeing to share the day with us. That's why Diana needed three days to get ready. She's helping the boys make gifts for everyone."

"Wow," Greg said softly, "what a great tradition. In this day and age, children are so used to being given to, they quickly come to expect it. But this is a wonderful way to teach them that it's better to give than receive."

"I thought so. Diana's teaching me and the boys so much about our heritage. There's a lot of good things about being Kolheek. About being Native American. Honor is important to Indians. As is loyalty. And there's a great respect for Elders as wise teachers of the young."

"Now, that's something children today could use a little more of," Sloan said. "Respect for their elders."

Greg snorted out a laugh. "Hey, buddy, your girls

are nearly teenagers, and everyone knows teenagers don't respect anyone.''

"They will," Travis quietly contradicted, "if they're taught that it's expected. Kids only do what's expected of them. If we expect little, that's exactly what they'll give us.''

"You learned all that from being a dad for a month?'' Sloan asked.

"It's been one long and laborious month.''

All three of them shared some light laughter. Then Travis had to admit, "It's Diana. She's taught me things that might have taken me a whole lifetime to learn.''

"Oh, Lord," Sloan muttered to Greg. "We know just how bad he's been bitten now that he's willing to credit Diana for his triumphs.''

Travis reached for the patient files that were up for discussion this morning, not wanting this meeting to turn into a teasing fest with him the main target attraction. "About the ceremony," he told them. "Dress warmly. Diana said we'll be outside." He cleared his throat. "Now, maybe we should get down to the work at hand.''

Greg reached out and grasped Travis's forearm, evidently reluctant to let the subject go. "Listen, pal. If you love Diana, then follow your heart. You'll find some way to reach her. I know you will.''

Travis was grateful for his friend's support. He only wished he had a small sliver of Greg's confidence.

The sky on New Year's Day was a clear blue. The air was brisk and dry. Much like the atmosphere between Travis and Diana since he'd kissed her in order to prove to her that she was a sensuous woman.

Oh, she'd been pleasant enough toward him when they were around the boys. But she remained aloof when the two of them were alone together. He'd tried several times to talk to her, but she refused to listen to anything he had to say.

She and the boys had spent their evenings threading colorful glass beads on strips of rawhide and sewing together simple leather pouches that they then decorated with shells and feathers they had purchased at the local craft store. When he'd asked her how she and the boys had occupied their days while he was at the office, she hadn't been forthcoming with much information. "Getting ready," had been all she had told him.

This morning, she'd made a strange request. She'd come in from outside and asked if she could take the decorations off the Christmas tree. After he'd helped her with the task, she, Josh and Jared had dragged the tree out beyond the stand of trees in the backyard. He had no idea what they had done with the pine tree, and when he'd asked the boys when they had come in for lunch, their eyes had glistened with an exciting secret. All they had said was, "You'll see." And they had hurried back outside after eating.

Now, the sun was about to set, their guests were expected to arrive very soon, and still there was no sign of Diana and the boys.

Travis's job was to make a meal to feed the guests after the ceremony. Diana had suggested something simple. Soup and sandwiches. Or something else that could be quickly reheated and set out after the festivities. The important part of this event would be the boys, not the food. Travis had chosen chili. The pot was simmering on the stove right now. And he'd purchased rolls at the local bakery. A crisp salad was in the refrigerator, ready to be served.

From the window, he spied Diana and the boys trudging from the woods carrying a shovel, an ax and other tools that they put away in the shed. His Medicine Woman looked so regal as she knelt down to talk to his children. Her departure would leave a hole in his heart. A huge hole.

Maybe, he thought, he could talk to her before the ceremony. Maybe he could make her understand… but rather than coming inside, Diana sent the boys in and then Travis watched her turn and walk back down the path they had worn in the snow.

Josh and Jared entered the back door, stomping the snow from their boots.

"Hey, Dad!" Jared greeted him, his cheeks red from the nippy weather. The child glowed with the obvious anticipation he felt. "Won't be long now."

Travis's heart lurched in his chest. He hadn't gotten used to hearing himself called Dad. But it seemed that his boys were getting more and more used to using the term.

"Wait a second," he called when they marched right past him. "Where are you going?"

"We have to wash up," Jared told him.

"And get dressed," Josh quietly added.

"Okay." They were antsy, and Travis didn't want to hold them up any longer. "If you need any help, just call me and I'll rush right up."

"Okay," they said, scrambling for the stairs in a flurry of sock-covered feet, knees and elbows.

Travis gave the chili one last stir before turning off the burner. It would reheat in just minutes when they were ready to eat. Moving into the dining room, he checked the table to see that everything was ready: plates, cutlery, glasses, napkins.

It wasn't long before the doorbell sounded, announcing some of the guests had arrived and were waiting at the front door. Travis had to smile when he saw that nearly everyone had arrived together: Jane, Greg and baby Joy, as well as Sloan, Sydney, Sophie and Sasha. And before the small crowd could even get inside, Rachel pulled her car into the driveway.

Hugs of greeting were made all-round and Travis then escorted the adults and children into the living room. They were still trying to decide whether or not to shed their coats when the boys entered the room. Their apparel made everyone go silent.

"We're ready," Jared proudly announced.

"B-but," Travis stumbled over the thoughts in his head, "I thought you were going to dress up in your best clothes."

Josh stepped forward shyly. "Diana told us to wear our very favorite stuff." Reaching inside his suit jacket, he rubbed the flat of his hand over his chest. "I never had soft pajamas. Neither has Jared. So we decided to wear our 'jama tops 'stead of our dress shirts."

Jared then took off his baseball cap and hugged it to him. "And, Dad, you gave me this Philly's hat back when I was in the hospital, 'member?"

Lifting his own cap, Josh said, "You brought me one, too."

"We love 'em."

Travis bit back the tears that splintered his gaze. His boys were precious, and if these articles of clothing were their favorites then he sure wasn't going to say otherwise.

"I think you look dashing," Jane said.

Rachel chimed in, "Quite handsome, indeed."

Jared ran to the window. "It's time. Diana said when we saw smoke, we would know it was time for us to come."

After the boys and Travis shrugged into their overcoats, the lot of them filed out the back door and down through the yard. The deciduous trees had lost their leaves weeks ago, but the towering pines were a vibrant green against the browns and grays of the early winter landscape. The salmon twilight of the setting sun lit their way.

"Why, look at that," Sophie, one of Sloan's daughters, called out. "It's a cute little fort."

"It's obviously a hut," Sasha informed her sister.

Sydney said, "You two are dweebs. Anyone can see, it's an igloo made of wood."

Sophie made a disgusted sound. "I'm no dweeb. And igloos are made of ice. Any idiot knows that."

Jared turned from where he was leading the group. "It's a wigwam. And me and Josh helped Diana build it."

"Ain't it cool?" Josh asked his dad.

Travis couldn't even nod an answer, he was so taken aback by what he saw. So this is what Diana and the boys had been doing while he was at work.

He smiled when he saw the boughs of their Christmas tree were being used to insulate the outside walls. Evidently she hadn't wanted to strip the precious trees on his property of their bark. The wigwam was just as Diana had helped him to imagine in his mind. To think, his forebears lived in dwellings such as this one. Shivers coursed across his skin like the hot points of a million stars rolling end over end.

After they exchanged a look, the boys focused their gazes on the doorway of the wigwam and shouted, "Hey!" Jared glanced at Travis and whispered, "That means hello."

"O'ho," Diana called back. "Welcome!"

Travis followed the boys inside, ducking his head in order to get through the doorway. The inside of the wigwam was toasty warm due to a small fire that had been built in a shallow pit in the middle of the floor. Wisps of smoke rose, escaping through the hole at the apex of the ceiling.

"Come in."

The sound of Diana's soft coaxing drew his gaze to her, and the sight of her made him stop in his tracks. Her ceremonial robe was made of supple white deer hide, the front of it decorated with elaborate beading. And the fluidlike fringe swept through the air with each movement of her hands and arms. Her black hair, left loose and flowing, glistened in the firelight. She was beautiful. Utterly and breathtakingly beautiful. It would have been easy for him imagine stepping back in time a thousand years.

Diana motioned to him and the others, and they all filed in. Then Sloan, the last to enter, folded down the blanket attached to the top of the doorway in order to hold in the heat. "Please, sit," she instructed them, and they all lowered themselves onto the mats and quilts she'd used to cover the bare earth floor.

Expectancy and anticipation seemed to ripple over the small group. Travis felt anxious nerves dancing in his stomach. Maybe that was because none of them really knew what to expect.

The sound of Diana's lyrical voice filled the air, and Travis's gaze riveted to her as she lifted her hands, palms open, in prayer. He wondered what the others might think of his magnificent Medicine Woman, yet he was too enamored with her at this moment to look at anyone or anything but her.

The Algonquian words rolled from her tongue like liquid gold, coating them all with the distinct feeling that this moment was sacred. Finally she let her gaze meet everyone in the wigwam and she greeted each person with a smile of true welcome.

"Tonight," she said, "you have graced us with your presence as we name Josh and Jared and Travis with their Kolheek names. But first, the boys have gifts for the ladies." She looked at the twins, then nodded at the boys.

"A long time ago," Jared haltingly began, "Indian girls would decorate their hair with beads made of seashells. Later, they had beads made of glass. The beads were sometimes used like money and it was called…" His words trailed as he looked at Diana with sudden panic. She smiled at him calmly.

Josh offered, "Wampum." He offered Sydney a string of colorful beads. "It's for decoration," he told her.

Sydney grinned with glee. "It's a hair clip," she

told her sisters as Jared handed the other girls theirs. The triplets thanked the boys and busied themselves inserting the clips into their hair.

"Back in the olden days, little girls played with dolls," Jared told Jane who was holding little Joy, "just like girls do today. So we made Joy a doll. It's felt, but sometimes the dolls were made of wood. But me and Josh don't know how to carve."

"It's beautiful," Jane told him. "Joy will cherish it." Joy's eyes were wide as she accepted the doll with its long hair made of strands of yarn.

Josh said, "We made purses for Jane and Rachel." The women smiled at him and he turned red.

Jared said, "These purses are better than what you buy in the store. They tie around your waist so you don't have to hold onto 'em." His tone was filled with fascination, as though he'd invented a brand-new idea.

Jane and Rachel oohed and aahed appreciatively over their gifts.

The boys then returned to the seats and Diana said, "I made the gifts for Sloan and Greg, but please remember, the gifts are given in honor of the boys and Travis." She twisted and when she turned to face them once again, Travis saw that she was holding two strips of fabric.

"Wampum belts were important to the Kolheek," she explained. "They were a record of history. Some wampum belts were a record of the laws. These belts I have made are of your personal history. As your history changes, the belts can change, too."

Greg received his belt with an indrawn breath. "It's just lovely, Diana. Thank you." Then he pointed to the beaded figures, saying to his wife, "Look, here's me, you and Joy."

"I'm on mine," Sloan said. "With the girls. Three of them. Identical triplets."

"Cool," one of the girls said.

"But, Diana," Greg said, "what's this symbol?"

"It represents a healer," she told him. "And the fringe on the bottom represents tendrils of smoke. Kolheek are The People Of The Smoke."

Everyone settled down quickly, but the excitement sparking in the warm air seemed to pop and snap with more energy as each second passed.

"As a Medicine Woman," Diana said, "it is my duty to get to know the boys well enough that I can bestow on them a name that fits them perfectly. Normally I do this by talking with their parents. However, that wasn't an available option to me since Travis was just getting to know the boys at the same time I was. So, I've spent lots and lots of time with them. We've talked about many things. I hope they have learned things from me, just as I have learned things from them."

Reaching out, she offered her hand to Jared, who took it and came to stand in front of where she sat.

"You will be called *GansXewulon kwan*," she told him. "Roaring Wing. Your wit is quick. Your communication skills powerful. I have watched you jump and play with great abandon. You will fly high and achieve many successes in your life."

Now it was Josh's turn to stand before the Medicine Woman. "Josh," she said, "you will be called *Kulamapuw Ox cho*. Quiet Mountain. Brother Mountain is loyal beyond belief, lending himself as refuge, year after year. He is honorable, loving those who come to dwell on him. And his vast age has granted him wisdom that is hard to equal. You, too, will achieve many successes in your life.''

Emotion knotted in Travis's throat. He would never be able to repay Diana for the pride she was helping to instill in Josh and Jared, for the memory she was providing his boys.

Diana asked both boys to stand and face the fire. All eyes were on the twins as Diana said, ''These children will require years of love and guidance if they are to grow into capable, strong and self-reliant adults. I ask you to grant these children the concern and affection that will instill in them a deep sense of security, and the firm direction that will enable them to grow into moral, responsible young men.''

Emphatic nods and murmurs of assent stirred the air. Then Diana paused, the wigwam once again growing silent, expectant. Closing her eyes, she sighed deeply. She rose and inched around behind Travis, placing her warm fingertips on his shoulders.

''For Travis, I have chosen the name *Xing wee E lah*. Great Warrior.''

Travis started with a jerk. He knew Diana had to have felt his reaction. But there was no way for him to see her face. Why would she gift him with such a name unless she'd had a change of heart? Unless she'd realized that the two of them belonged together...

''No one,'' Diana calmly continued, ''but the greatest of warriors would come to the aid of two sick little boys. No one but the greatest of warriors would go to the lengths that Travis has for Josh and

Jared. Rescuing them when they were lost. Taking them in. Loving them. Providing for them. When they had no one else."

With each word she spoke, Travis felt a little more deflated. He'd thought the name she'd given him had to do with her feelings for him. With their feelings for each other. However, he quickly realized that wasn't what she'd been thinking at all.

He was proud of his Kolheek name. He was proud to be seen, to be thought of, as having saved the boys. But that concept went both ways. Those children had saved him. They had helped to open a whole new world to him. They had brought the bright and warm light of love into his cold, dim life. For that, he would be forever grateful. He loved his boys. Very much.

"I know that all of you here love Travis," she said to the group. "During my time in Philadelphia, I have seen the deep friendships all of you share. All I ask, is that you continue to support Travis. Continue to love him. Continue to be his friends."

Emotions ran high in the small confines of the wigwam. The eyes of every female were misty with tears. Even the men seemed choked up by the warm sentiment Diana had created.

The feelings churning in Travis were phenomenal. Pride and love for his boys roared through him like a raging river. Appreciation, affection and joy rushed at him when he gazed at all his friends. Yet a deep sadness squirmed inside him when he thought of losing the love of his life.

Later that evening when the house was quiet, Diana stood in the living room, staring out at the night.

Clouds had begun to gather and snow was falling, softly, silently.

The guests had left, the boys were sleeping, and she had no idea where Travis was. But she knew he hadn't gone to bed. She knew he intended to speak with her. She had read it in the deep, intense looks he'd given her through dinner.

She hadn't wanted to tell him the full truth. She hadn't wanted him to know that she wasn't a whole woman. But in the end, she was sure he'd force her into it. She was sure he wouldn't stop trying to convince her that they were meant to be together until she revealed all there was to reveal. The thought made her melancholy. But she could tell revealing all would be inevitable.

Besides, what did it matter if he knew? She'd be leaving here. And she'd never see Travis again.

That thought was enough to make her eyes mist.

"Diana."

She closed her eyes. It was time. She'd have to tell him.

"Please don't be angry with me any longer," he said. "I know now that I should never have kissed you that way. I should never have tried to…"

His words faded. It was clear that his heart was aching. But there was nothing she could do about that. There was nothing she could do about the ache in her own heart. "I'm not angry anymore," she told him. "I do understand that you meant well. I know that now."

"But you still don't understand that we're soul mates, do you? You still intend to leave."

She sighed then, and turned to face him. "I will tell you the truth, Travis. I believe that..." Her breath caught. Did she really have the courage to say this? "I believe that we are soul mates. But I still intend to leave."

"But *why?*"

He touched her then, his palms cupping her shoulders, and hot tears welled in her eyes. She hated seeing the hurt in his eyes, hated knowing that she put it there. "I have proof," she told him. "Evidence of my...condition."

"Evidence? What are you talking about?"

Her inhalation was shaky. "All those months I was married. I never had an...I never..."

"Climaxed?" he offered. "You've never had an orgasm?"

She nodded, unable to look him in the eye. "If I stayed here, if we were to be together, our relationship would fall apart faster than you can imagine. Frustration is a terrible thing for a man to have to suffer. I know. I've seen it before." Forcing herself to look up into his face, she added, "I would never want to see you look at me with anger and disappointment. Never. That's why I'm leaving. Tomorrow." With sorrow weighing heavy on her, she turned from him and walked away.

Hours later, she lay awake, desolation covering her in a mantle colder and more suffocating than the inches of snow that had fallen. What would her grandmother say? she wondered. How would her grandmother respond to Diana's returning to the reservation, once again, brokenhearted.

It was then that her grandmother's odd words

came back to echo in her mind: *We'll see what fate has in store.*

Diana sat up in bed. Could her grandmother have known? she wondered. Could her grandmother have realized that she was going to fall in love with Travis?

The knock on her bedroom door had her glancing at the clock: 2:00 a.m. The last thing she wanted was more discussion about her sexual dysfunction. She covered her head and hoped he'd go away. Long minutes ticked by without a second knock. Why would he…?

Curiosity made her toss back the covers and go to the door. She pulled it open. The hallway was empty, but taped to the outside of the door was a note. Peering in the moonlight, she read, *Meet me in the wigwam.*

Oh, Lord, he was going to make her refuse him yet again. Tugging on her boots, she wearily tied the laces and pulled the quilt off the bed to use as a cloak. This wouldn't take long.

Moonlight lit a path through the bare trees and threw shadows over the snow. She shivered, but trudged ahead. Pulling aside the blanket covering the doorway, she ducked and went inside.

"Travis…"

The wigwam was empty, a fire casting an orange glow and plenty of warmth. She let the quilt drop to the floor. Where was he?

The question barely had time to register in her mind when she heard it. The soulful notes of a flute. Travis was serenading her! The idea was so romantic, so heartwarming, that she had to smile. The man was impossible. Unwittingly she knelt down on the quilt to listen to the simple tune. What it told her was that he wanted her despite her problem. That he loved her enough to want her just the way she was. Her heart swelled with warmth.

The music ended, and his handsome face appeared in the doorway. "Okay," he said, "so I don't have much musical talent."

Despite the dire situation, she laughed.

He came inside, sliding down next to her. "That's the most beautiful sound I've ever heard. Prettier than any flute. Any flute I've ever played, anyway."

"You're so silly," she said.

"But you love me," he whispered. "Say it. I want to hear you say it."

"Oh, Travis." She tried to look away, but he captured her chin between his gentle fingers. Finally, she admitted, "I do. I love you. But—"

"No buts. Trust me."

"I want to, but—"

"Now, now," he warned, a delicious twinkle glittering in his dark gaze, "what did I say about that?"

His kissed her then. Soundly. Sensuously. Seductively.

"Do you know how happy I am?" he asked. "To know that your first time…your first fulfillment will be with me?"

"But how can you be sure…?"

He shook his head. "There's that *b* word again."

His lips on her face, on her neck, sent heated tendrils curling down low in her gut. His hands roved over her waist, her hips, her back.

"Diana, your ex-husband was an fool. A selfish

jerk who didn't concern himself with your happiness. He didn't take the time to satisfy you. I know it. I feel it. Down deep in my soul.''

He placed another kiss high on her breast and she was barely able to stifle a moan. The heated creepers inside her writhed and twirled. Never before had she experienced such feelings.

''Now—'' he paused long enough to rain soft kisses along the curve of her neck ''—a soul mate's primary focus is the satisfaction of his lover.''

''Primary…'' The word came out sounding breathy. ''Focus…''

''Mmm-hmm.''

He kissed her, touched her, everywhere…until Diana thought she'd lose her mind. She wanted to trust him. Wanted him to be the love of her life. Her white knight. Her soul mate. She wanted desperately for him to satisfy her in every way possible.

And he did.

Right then.

Right there.

Later, they stroked and caressed each other, the luminescence of the fire's embers turning their bodies coppery. ''We should go in,'' he whispered against her ear. ''The boys might wake.''

She nodded, but held him back when he made to rise. ''I need to tell you something.''

''What is it?''

Chagrin heated her cheeks. ''I have to be honest. About your name.''

''My Kolheek name?''

She nodded. ''What you've done for the boys is wonderful,'' she told him. ''But I chose your name—'' reaching up, she lay her palm against his jaw lovingly ''—because you're the great warrior who conquered my unconquerable heart.''

She had trusted him. And in him she'd found an honorable man. A lover. A friend. A man with whom she could find true happiness. In him she had found her Great Warrior.

* * * * *

*Will Sloan ever see what's
right before his eyes?
Join Donna Clayton and the*
SINGLE DOCTOR DADS
next month to find out!

RACHEL AND THE M.D.

*In stores December 2000,
only from Silhouette Romance!*

Coming soon from
Silhouette Romance...

SINGLE DOCTOR DADS

A captivating
new miniseries from

DONNA CLAYTON

*Changed by fatherhood...
healed by love!*

Meet three dashing doctors who share a bustling medical practice...and set pulses racing with their smoldering good looks. These gorgeous physicians could use some TLC of their own when they tackle single fatherhood! What is the perfect prescription for what ails these needy new dads? Why, a hefty dose of soul-searing romance might be just what the doctor ordered....

You won't want to miss a moment of
this irresistible new series:

THE NANNY PROPOSAL
(SR #1477, on sale October 2000)

THE DOCTOR'S MEDICINE WOMAN
(SR #1483, on sale November 2000)

RACHEL AND THE M.D.
(SR #1489, on sale December 2000)

Available at your favorite retail outlet.

Silhouette®

Where love comes alive™

Visit Silhouette at www.eHarlequin.com   SRSDD

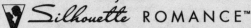

You're not going to believe this offer!

**In October and November 2000, buy any two Harlequin
or Silhouette books and save $10.00 off future purchases,
or buy any three and save $20.00 off future purchases!**

Just fill out this form and attach 2 proofs of purchase (cash register
receipts) from October and November 2000 books and Harlequin will
send you a coupon booklet worth a total savings of $10.00 off future
purchases of Harlequin and Silhouette books in 2001. Send us 3 proofs
of purchase and we will send you a coupon booklet worth a total
savings of $20.00 off future purchases.

Saving money has never been this easy.

I accept your offer! Please send me a coupon booklet:

Name: _____

Address: _____ City: _____

State/Prov.: _____ Zip/Postal Code: _____

Optional Survey!

In a typical month, how many Harlequin or Silhouette books would you buy <u>new</u> at retail stores?

☐ Less than 1   ☐ 1   ☐ 2   ☐ 3 to 4   ☐ 5+

Which of the following statements best describes how you <u>buy</u> Harlequin or Silhouette books?
Choose one answer only that <u>best</u> describes you.

☐ I am a regular buyer and reader

☐ I am a regular reader but buy only occasionally

☐ I only buy and read for specific times of the year, e.g. vacations

☐ I subscribe through Reader Service but also buy at retail stores

☐ I mainly borrow and buy only occasionally

☐ I am an occasional buyer and reader

Which of the following statements best describes how you <u>choose</u> the Harlequin and Silhouette
series books you buy <u>new</u> at retail stores? By "series," we mean books within a particular line,
such as *Harlequin PRESENTS* or *Silhouette SPECIAL EDITION*. Choose one answer only that
<u>best</u> describes you.

☐ I only buy books from my favorite series

☐ I generally buy books from my favorite series but also buy
books from other series on occasion

☐ I buy some books from my favorite series but also buy from
many other series regularly

☐ I buy all types of books depending on my mood and what
I find interesting and have no favorite series

Please send this form, along with your cash register receipts as proofs of purchase, to:
In the U.S.: Harlequin Books, P.O. Box 9057, Buffalo, NY 14269
In Canada: Harlequin Books, P.O. Box 622, Fort Erie, Ontario L2A 5X3
(Allow 4-6 weeks for delivery) Offer expires December 31, 2000.

PHQ4002

where love comes alive—online...

eHARLEQUIN.com

shop eHarlequin

- ♥ Find all the new Silhouette releases at everyday great discounts.
- ♥ Try before you buy! Read an excerpt from the latest Silhouette novels.
- ♥ Write an online review and share your thoughts with others.

reading room

- ♥ Read our Internet exclusive daily and weekly online serials, or vote in our interactive novel.
- ♥ Talk to other readers about your favorite novels in our Reading Groups.
- ♥ Take our Choose-a-Book quiz to find the series that matches you!

authors' alcove

- ♥ Find out interesting tidbits and details about your favorite authors' lives, interests and writing habits.
- ♥ Ever dreamed of being an author? Enter our Writing Round Robin. The Winning Chapter will be published online! Or review our writing guidelines for submitting your novel.

If you enjoyed what you just read,
then we've got an offer you can't resist!

Take 2 bestselling love stories FREE!

Plus get a FREE surprise gift!

ATTENTION **JOAN JOHNSTON** FANS!

Silhouette Books is proud to present

HAWK'S WAY
BACHELORS

The first three novels in
the bestselling Hawk's Way series
now in one fabulous collection!

On Sale December 2000

THE RANCHER AND THE RUNAWAY BRIDE
Brawny rancher Adam Phillips has his hands full when
Tate Whitelaw's overprotective, bossy brothers show up with
shotguns in hand!

THE COWBOY AND THE PRINCESS
Ornery cowboy Faron Whitelaw is caught off-guard
when breathtakingly beautiful Belinda Prescott proves to be
more than a gold digger!

THE WRANGLER AND THE RICH GIRL
Sparks fly when Texas debutante Candy Baylor makes handsome
horse breeder Garth Whitelaw an offer he can't refuse!

**HAWK'S WAY: Where the Whitelaws of Texas
run free…till passion brands their hearts.**

"Joan Johnston does contemporary Westerns to perfection."
—Publishers Weekly

Available at your favorite retail outlet.

Where love comes alive™

Visit Silhouette at www.eHarlequin.com   PSHWB

#1 *New York Times* bestselling author

NORA ROBERTS

introduces the loyal and loving, tempestuous and tantalizing Stanislaski family.

Coming in November 2000:

The Stanislaski Brothers

Mikhail and Alex

Their immigrant roots and warm, supportive home had made Mikhail and Alex Stanislaski both strong and passionate. And their charm makes them irresistible....

In February 2001, watch for
THE STANISLASKI SISTERS: Natasha and Rachel

And a brand-new Stanislaski story from Silhouette Special Edition,
CONSIDERING KATE

Available at your favorite retail outlet.

Where love comes alive™